# PARADISE SQUARE

# PARADISE SQUARE

## E.M. SCHORB

**HILL HOUSE**          **NEW YORK**

ISBN: 978-0-578-52906-6

Cover Art:  Brenda Pinnell
Cover Design:  Selah Bunzey

# INTRODUCTION

Many mystery fans know that the father of the genre was none other than Edgar Allen Poe. In *Paradise Square*, a remarkable novel by E.M. Schorb set in the 19th century, Poe himself assists in the investigation of a young woman's murder. This thrilling and satisfying work, which won the Grand Prize at the Frankfurt Ebook Awards, delves into the mystery of the killer's identity and also explores the spotty record surrounding the end of Poe's career when he disappeared and was later found dying, apparently as a result of a drinking binge.

Schorb brings Poe to vivid life as he joins Officer Goode—a 'leatherhead' as municipal patrolmen were nicknamed for the thick helmets they wore—in investigating the grisly slaying of a street vendor. Initially recruited to clear the name of a West Point friend, Poe is drawn by his fascination with mystery and deduction into aiding the inexperienced officer. Goode himself, who owes his appointment to political connections, suspects his assignment to the case is based largely on his inexperience, and that he was never intended to learn the killer's identity.

Throughout the novel, Schorb inventively finds ways to mention true aspects of Poe's life. The reader learns that he attended West Point but left after too much gambling and drinking, that his parents were actors, and that his name, if not face, garnered instant recognition among the literate then, just as it does today. More impressively, Poe's character transcends factual details and achieves life as a brilliant, haunted Southern gentleman.

The novel's title refers to a tiny square in a New York slum where the murder victim was found. Events radiate from this locale, encompassing many little-known aspects of the slums of a young New York. The reader joins Poe and Officer Goode in exploring the squalid taverns or 'diving bells'—known today as 'dives'—of the slums, the homes of reformers and the lodges of some of the many groups that are at once social club, street gang, and political clique.

In 19th-Century New York, where these gangs exerted powerful influence, even fire service was provided by rival groups. In an amusing episode, Poe intervenes to prevent a member of one gang from obstructing a fire hydrant's use by another gang crew. This small taste of ruthlessness and rivalry foreshadows the lengths to which these gangs will go to maintain their control. Like the House of Usher looming over its moor, the specter of the corrupt Tammany Hall political machine casts its shadow over the pair's investigation.

By mixing elements of the historical novel and the conventional mystery with a speculative reconstruction of Poe's final days, Schorb has crafted a fascinating tale. He does great honor to Poe's memory and fame as the father of the genre. The scribe would be pleased with his protegee's work.

—Gregory Harris, *BookPage.com*

*for Patricia*

*About what happened during the days of which we have no record we can believe anything we choose, including either that Poe had spent his time in a drunken debauch or that he did not drink anything at all. Extant testimonials simply cancel each other out, and there is no way, at this date, to determine who is telling the truth.*

Edward Wagenknecht
*Edgar Allan Poe*
*The Man Behind the Legend*

# Chapter 1

## I FIND POE

I found Edgar Poe at the Old Brewery, seated at a table in a taper-lit, basement room, his large head resting on his folded arms, in a drunken, obviously troubled sleep.

It had not been difficult to find him. I had simply followed the trail of the "reciting poet" from diving bell to diving bell, as these basement rum-parlors are called, at the last of which it had been overheard that he, in company with "some other Irishmen," was going to the Old Brewery to pass the night. The "other Irishmen" may have been those who slept noisily at the table with Poe.

Apparently, he had not been robbed or brutalized, probably because he did not look like a man who had any money. He was unshaven and dirty, his suit threadbare and his linen soiled. An unpromising picture of a man in whom Peter VanBrunt, and, to a lesser degree, I myself, had placed hope.

# Chapter 2

## THE FIVE POINTS

The intersection of Anthony, Little Water, Cross, Orange, and Mulberry Streets gave the name Five Points to New York's most infamous slum. At the center of this intersection was Paradise Square, a fenced-in plot of sparse grass and caked mud serving the purpose of a small park. If Paradise Square was the geographical center of the Five Points, the Old Brewery was its dark heart. One block north of Paradise Square, it was built as Coulter's Brewery in 1792, and became famous in the eastern states for its brew. By 1837, it was abandoned, and claimed by squatters, eventually housing over a thousand men, women, and children, black and white, a large proportion of whom had no other means to earn their sparse living but by gambling, harlotry, thievery and violence. It averaged a murder a night. Seldom were the murderers brought to book. The police did not have the numbers required for an invasion of such a thug-infested tenement.

The Municipal Police, even patrolmen, wore no uniforms at this time, a policy I was to play a part in changing, but that served the purpose of anonymity at the moment. I had pocketed my copper star, which I sometimes wore pinned to my breast pocket, even though I had lately been assigned as a detective, and had no need to wear it, and had been as careful as possible to be inconspicuous. A copper caught in the Old Brewery had little chance of leaving it alive. I reached

3

across the table and tapped Poe on the shoulder. He jerked awake like a man to whom healthy sleep is unknown. I spoke in a whisper.

"Mr. Poe?"

"Yes, I think so," he said, rubbing his eyes. "In any case, his remains."

"I am Sergeant Jonathan Goode of the Municipal Police," I said, and quickly stated my business. When Poe had heard enough, he gathered himself and followed me out through the catacomb-like passages of the Old Brewery.

Outside, I could see the damage Poe had done himself.

I knew him to be between thirty-five and forty years of age; but, at the moment, he looked much older. He was ashen, his gray restless eyes shot with a web of hemorrhaged veins. He was a bit below middle height, but carried his sturdy physique in a military manner, and could not be described as a small man. His temples and forehead were remarkably prominent; his mouth and jaw determined, decisive. He wore black from hat to heel. Hat, frockcoat, gloves, and boots had seen better days, but "gentleman" was written all over him.

I knew he must be attended before we could proceed to our business.

"We'll get you a room at Red Kate's Emerald Isle. Mr. VanBrunt stays there. You can get a meal, a bath, and a change of linen. Unless, of course, you have a place."

4

"I believe I had one, but I can't remember where. In any case, I doubt if I should be welcomed back."

If I may ask, sir, where have you been sleeping?"

"On tables, I should think—or under them. I have no money, I'm afraid."

"I'll tend to everything, Mr. Poe, and you can repay me when you're able."

"That's very good of you, Sergeant. Yes, I shall go to my publisher. He'll have royalties for me." He did not seem very positive about this.

I liked his voice. It was of middle range, and possessed of a soft Southern accent.

This was Wednesday, just before noon, November 15th, 1847, a cold, drizzling day, and one that I shall never forget. I was wearing my mackintosh. Poe did not seem to notice the rain any more than did the swarming rats, cats, dogs, pigs, horses, or suffering humanity of the Five Points.

# Chapter 3

## THE EMERALD ISLE

There were scores of dance houses in the Five Points, but Red Kate's Emerald Isle was unusual, if not unique, in being a hotel-boarding house on its upper stories and a dance hall-saloon at street level. It was an emerald-green clapboard building, with windows ornamented in red bombazine. From the saloon ceiling hung hoop chandeliers filled with candles. Sand was liberally distributed on the dance floor to afford better footing for heavy boots. Time had no meaning in the Five Points, for regularity of employment did not exist for the great mass of its denizens, and the music never stopped in the dance houses. Morning, noon, and night, the hornpipe and fiddle bit at drunken ears and gave rhythm to the staggering. As we approached, the lively fiddle strains of "The Land of the Potato O" could be heard emanating from within.

"I know this place," said Poe. "I've been here. In fact, it was here that I ran into VanBrunt. I remember now that he said something about getting married. Was he speaking of the murdered girl?"

"Yes, sir, I believe he must have been."

Poe took the lead and made his way through the crowd to the oaken bar.

6

Red Kate was a plump, pretty woman in her late thirties, henna-haired, with a wide-eyed, bow-lipped face, and rough voice, who had started out as something under a cab moll, or madam, and worked her way up to something like legitimacy. It was said that she could be violent to the point of ferocity when crossed. Behind her was a large glass jar, on hideous display, containing ears which, it was said, Kate had bitten from the heads of difficult customers. She was busy with a customer up the bar.

I gave Poe the chance to down a beer and a few free black sturgeon caviar sandwiches, and called Kate over.

"'Lo, copper!"

"Hello, Kate. I'd like you to meet Mr. Edgar Allan Poe, the writer. He's a friend of Mr. VanBrunt's. He's going to try to help him."

"I met Mr. Poe, but he probably don't remember. He was with Peter on Saturday night, and something the worse for wear."

"Madam." Poe attempted to click his rundown heels, and nodded his head in a courtly bow.

"Mr. Poe needs a room—and some tending."

"*No-Nose!*" Red Kate boomed over the dance-house din, "*No-Nose Mullins!*" In a moment, a long haired, black-bearded giant emerged from the dancers on the floor.

Poe was self-possessed in not showing the shock everyone felt when first confronted with No-Nose Mullins. In place of the missing feature, the huge bouncer wore a scrimshanked ivory nose, held in place by two cat-gut thongs tied behind his neck and head. He was Kate's bodyguard and general factotum.

"Yes, ma'am," he said, presenting himself.

"Take Mr. Poe here to a room, get him a tub of hot water, let him bathe, shave, give him a massage, and when he's ready, I'll send up some food. Take a bottle of good rum and some glasses along."

I saw rebellion flicker in Poe's eyes, and his firm jaw set; but Kate knew her men. The "bottle of good rum" mollified him.

"I am in your debt, madam." Poe bowed and followed Mullins into the upper regions of the place.

"Can he help?" Kate asked doubtfully.

"You can't judge a poet by his boots, Kate."

Kate and I had a lunch of pigs' feet, boiled potatoes, bread, and beer. The food at the Emerald Isle was very bad, but for me that day it was on the house, so I didn't complain, and contented myself while eating with listening to Red Kate sing—

> *Faith, if such was my lot,*
> *Little Ireland's the spot*
> *Where I'd build my snug cot,*
> *With a bit of garden to it O!*

8

*And I'd ne'er places come,*
*Nor abroad ever roam*
*But enjoy my sweet home*
*In the land of the potato O . . .*

Within the hour we joined Poe in his room. A bath had put some color in his face, and the rum had animated him.

Kate seemed to find his rugged, Celtic good looks, and courtly, Southern manner attractive. In a half-hour, she told him to call her Kate and asked if she could call him Eddie.

"Indeed, Kate," he said, "all my friends call me Eddie."

"Sir, are you prepared to hear more of the circumstances of the murder?"

Poe drew on a slim green cheroot. Smoke swirling about his head, he said:

"Fire away, Sergeant!"

# Chapter 4

## THE HIDEOUS MURDER OF THE HOT CORN GIRL

"The details are as follows, sir. The victim was a Hot Corn Girl. Perhaps you've seen them, vending corn on the cob. They appear around dusk, and mingle with the crowds on the sidewalks and in the dance houses. They're on the streets until late November, the end of harvest season. Some of the girls are followed by young bloods who hurl brickbats at any cove who dares to flirt with them. Mary Hart, the victim, apparently had no such champion. She entered Paradise Square, and, in a matter of seconds, a scream was heard. Mr. VanBrunt was discovered kneeling over her body, holding a cleaver. A short time before, he was at the bar downstairs, drunk, and saying that he intended to propose to her. He had been seeing her for some time. *He* says, that, after leaving here, he made his way, with a few stops at diving bells, to Paradise Square. The Square has a fence around it and, as you may have noticed, sir, the women in the neighborhood use it as a clothes-line, thus generally blocking any view of the interior. There are two entrances to the park, one to the east and one to the west. He says that as he approached the east gate he heard a scream, and ran the remaining few yards into the Square, where he found Mary Hart, in a butchered condition, the cleaver by her side.

"There was a gang of street urchins at the east entrance. They gather there constantly and collect a bit of change from the women for guarding the laundry, and spend their time dicing and fighting over the spoils. The only witness to

10

come forward is a clubfooted boy who seems to have no other name than the 'Gimp.' He's a hardcase of about sixteen. Most of the boys are much younger. I imagine the Gimp hangs about to take advantage of the younger boys. He's a cruel little brute who tortures animals. As a patrolman, I've had occasion to caution him on that. In any case, the others ran off at the first stir of trouble. Apparently, the Gimp's deformed foot prevented him from taking a similar flight. He says that he heard a scream, looked in at the west gate, where he alone had been posted, and saw Mr. Van-Brunt."

Poe mused for a moment, then said: "What exactly is it that you wish me to do, Sergeant?"

I asked to speak with Poe in private. When Red Kate and Mullins had gone downstairs, I said:

"It was Mr. VanBrunt who suggested that I enlist your aid, sir. He said you would help him—and me."

"I owe Peter VanBrunt a great debt. He and I were classmates at West Point."

"He told me that, sir."

"Did he tell you the circumstances?"

"No, sir."

"I was forced to leave West Point under a cloud. There were social obligations at the Point, and I was unable to meet them because my stepfather did not give me an adequate allowance. I refused to attend classes until my allowance

11

was increased. He refused to increase it, though it was clearly inadequate, and I was expelled. I had bills, and had had to borrow from other cadets. Peter pressed a sum upon me, so that I could pay back the others, and not leave feeling that I'd abused anyone's friendship. I regret to say, I've never been in a position to repay him. Yes, Sergeant, I'm certainly willing to help Peter VanBrunt. But why do *you* need my help?"

"Well, sir, it requires a bit of an explanation. Would you do me the honor of hearing me out?"

"Please proceed."

I hesitated as to how to proceed, then plunged on as best I could. "One day I was hunting quail in New Jersey with my cousin, and he asked me if I'd like to take his place as a leatherhead—"

"A leatherhead?"

"A patrolman. Down here in the Five Points we wear leather helmets, our only uniform. Somebody's always throwing a brickbat at you. My cousin was going to quit, having come upon a profitable venture, and 'Boss' Meade, the alderman of this ward, the Sixth, fondly known as 'the Butcher' because he began his career as one, had given him the chance to name his successor. Aldermen nominate men from their districts. Well, I had no work, and thought I might as well carry a club until something better came along. When my cousin resigned, I was sworn in. Then I learned that my cousin had paid Meade a hundred dollars to set me up, and that such bribes are common practice. Furthermore, my cousin had paid double the usual rate of fifty dollars to by-

12

pass the residency laws, which state that a police candidate has to have resided in the area where he is to work for at least five years, and has to remain in that district after appointment. I had never set foot in the Five Points, and still live in Greenwich Village. Though nowhere near of your caliber, sir, I am a literate man, and harbor a hope yet of someday writing something worth while."

"The writing life is a harder one than you may imagine," said Poe. "But carry on."

"I've paid my cousin back, but I feel as if I've paid a bribe at second hand."

Poe said: "But Sergeant, you still haven't answered my question."

"I am by way of answering it, sir. If you'll bear with me. . ."

Poe nodded, puffing thoughtfully at his cheroot.

"I was thrown on to patrol without any instructions as to my duties, merely ordered to report to Captain Henchard of the Sixth Ward Station on Anthony Street. Until yesterday morning I was a patrol sergeant. All this is by way of saying, sir, that there are no examinations required to be a Municipal Policeman, no attention whatever paid to the physique or mental qualities of the applicant. Service is for a term of two years, of which I've barely completed one. As for detailment for detective work, which is more healthy than pounding a beat in all kinds of weather, that comes at the whim of the captains, who usually select their favorites for it. In sum, sir, I suspect that I've been put on this case for the very reason that I am *not* qualified, and I resent it. I don't like being used. More, I've seen Mr. VanBrunt around, on the streets and here at Red Kate's, and I cannot believe he's guilty. The idea of such a man using a cleaver on a young woman is not to be believed. He's a gentleman." I didn't know quite how to put the next bit, so I just blundered ahead. "I've always believed your analysis of the murder of Mary Rogers, in 'The Mystery of Marie Roget,' to be correct. Naturally, when Mr. VanBrunt suggested that I seek your help, I leaped at the opportunity."

"Let me ask you this, Sergeant. Is there no more experienced detective at your station who could help you?"

"As I say, sir, I believe I've been chosen because I am *not* experienced, and so can expect no help from anyone at the station."

"Would you care to explain more fully?"

"There are political implications, sir. Mr. VanBrunt is a friend of Miss Kate's and Miss Kate is no friend of Boss Meade."

"Ah. What about a lawyer? Does VanBrunt have one?"

I laughed. "Kate sent hers to Anthony Street, and Captain Henchard locked him up, saying he was drunk. Now he's in the cell next to Mr. VanBrunt's. I've been told they can't wake him up. He may have been beaten."

Poe said, "Let's beard the lion," and rose to his feet.

Downstairs, at the bar, we stopped to speak with Kate.

"Have you been to see Peter?" Poe asked her.

"Captain Henchard wouldn't let me see him."

Poe shook his head and dropped his cheroot in a spittoon.

Red Kate said: "Peter didn't kill that girl, Eddie. He's just a party balloon filled with a wind of blarney. It was the drink that made him think he was young again, and in love with a girl half his age."

"I understand," said Poe, but there was a cast of doubt in his gray eyes.

"Wait now," said Kate. "I think you should take my man Mullins along. The Sergeant's a greenhorn in the Five Points. If you mean to go on with this, Mullins'll be useful. He can get you in where you wouldn't be let, and get people to talk to you as would develop a case of lockjaw if they thought they was talking to coppers."

# Chapter 5

## WEST POINT TIES

At the Anthony Street station, VanBrunt sat dejectedly on the plank bunk of his damp, basement cell. He was a long thin grizzled blond with watery pale eyes, aquiline nose, and a parted goatee. He was also a former army officer, and at one time a promising magazine illustrator, who had gone to seed, abetted by personal demons. Greeting him, Poe gave his shoulder a push. "Look, I've come to help, as you requested. Try to lift your spirits. Think of our times at Benny Havens' tavern in Highland Falls. He said to me, "I used to call Benny the sole congenial soul at West Point. Of course, that was before Peter befriended me." He gave VanBrunt a wink. "You remember: *We'll sing our reminiscences of Benny Havens, Oh!* You know," he said, turning to me again, "it is the custom for each class to add a stanza to the song before graduation. It must be getting interminable. *Oh, we'll sing our reminiscences of Benny Havens, Oh!* Now, I promise you, Peter, you are not going to die for a murder you did not commit. In the spirit of Benny Havens I have brought you a gift." Poe took the bottle of rum from his coat and gave it to him. VanBrunt seized upon it, taking several breathless drafts. I had not known about the rum. It was strictly forbidden; but I said nothing. Poe was right. VanBrunt needed it.

"Why hasn't Kate come to see me?" he asked, wiping his mouth.

16

"She tried," I said. "Captain Henchard wouldn't allow it. But I think if she were to try again—now—he'd relent. He knows your background by now."

"Well," VanBrunt persisted, not fully taking in what I had said, "why hasn't she sent a lawyer?"

"She did send her lawyer. He came in drunk, and Captain Henchard locked him up. But I believe he may be willing to release him now. You see, sir, a journalist named McNeil wrote the murder up. He described you as being from an in-fluential family. That changed things. Boss Meade probably would have let you rot otherwise. Captain Henchard told me that your case should be handled gingerly."

"In other words," said Poe, "Meade and Henchard became willing to put an inexperienced detective on the case, to show that something was being done."

"Yes, sir. You see my position. Fortunately," I directed to VanBrunt, "the officer who arrested you only brought you in on suspicion, and that's all you're being held on."

"What about bail?" asked Poe.

"We have no station house bail, as they do in London, sir—a policy we should emulate. Besides, it wouldn't apply in the case of suspicion, particularly suspicion of murder. But we can only hold a suspect for five days without charging him."

VanBrunt downed another draft of rum. Letting the bottle drop into his lap, he said:

"But, Eddie, you haven't asked me if I'm guilty."

17

"I know you and therefore know that you are not. But say it, if you wish."

"I am innocent."

"You loved her?"

"To know her was to love her, Eddie. She came from a decent shopkeeper's family, but she was too young to have enjoyed its value when misfortune struck. Her father lost his business, and died soon after. Her mother, a blind woman, came upon unimaginable hard times with widowhood. Mary was reared, along with a sister, in poverty. But she never lost her fineness. You *must* find her murderer, Eddie, not just to free me, nor even to clear my name, but to punish the fiend that could harm so dear and lovely a girl."

"Where—*how* did you meet her?"

He shrugged. "It's lost to me now. For years I've been soaking my mind in rum for the express purpose of forgetting. Perhaps I talked to her first in Red Kate's, when she was vending—perhaps it was on the street. I don't remember."

"What is it you are trying to forget?"

"Ah, Eddie. . . everything! You should have had the money, you had the talent. But the money's tainted. My ancestors were cruel, greedy, and stupid, and my guilt at being descended from such men has plagued my life. They killed the red man for his land and scalped him to sell his hair in Europe. It was Dutch trappers who taught the Indian to take scalps. They sold Indian scalps to the Europeans like a kind

18

of novelty fur. And then these sons and grandsons of scalpers, these rich and respectable murderers, disowned me because I left the military to be an artist. I have an artist's sensitive temperament. I drank to forget. And now what character I do have has been weakened by my aimless Bohemian life.

"As for Mary, at first I entertained thoughts of seduction with regard to her, but she soon made clear to me that, though not of my so-called exalted origins, she was nevertheless of that natural nobility which would not enter into a dishonorable intrigue. She avowed her love for me, but held that love must prove itself elevating of its object, or be proven false to itself. In short, she challenged me to rise to the lofty, to abjure drink, and to consider marriage. I told you, though you may not remember, as I told everyone at Red Kate's, that I intended to propose marriage. But was that Saturday, or was it Sunday, or Monday?"

"You may have told me on Saturday," said Poe. "I'm not too clear on that myself."

"It was Monday evening," said Mullins, who was standing by. "I was there."

"Monday? The thing is, I was trying—trying to convince myself, perhaps—that I could live up to her idea of my ultimate decency. That's right. We had an appointment to meet in Paradise Square on Monday evening."

I said, "Theory has it that you kept your appointment, made your proposal, which she refused, and murdered her while in a drunken rage."

"No, *no!* I made my announcement, left Red Kate's, stopped at a few diving bells to strengthen my resolve, and went to meet her. As I approached that verminous little plot, I heard a scream. You can't see into the place, Eddie, for all the laundry on the fence, and it was dark. I ran and found her, an angel, butchered like an animal. Oh, God! But we've gone through this before, Sergeant. Don't you believe me?"

"Were there others who saw this," asked Poe—"Heard her *scream* before *you* entered?"

"There was a group of little toughs, dicing." He looked at me. "Have you questioned them?"

"By the time the officer came," I said, "they were part of a crowd. We don't know which boys were there at the time of the murder. We only have the Gimp for witness."

"Is there no way," Poe asked me, "to get Peter out of this dungeon?"

"Oh, yes, sir. Under the Municipal Code, an alderman, who is, ex-officio, a magistrate, can discharge a prisoner. But, to be frank, sir, aldermen generally only release their political supporters without an investigation. And, as I've said, Boss Meade doesn't look with favor on Red Kate—or any friend of hers."

"What is the nature of the animosity between Boss Meade and Red Kate?"

I don't know, sir. It appears to go back a long way. But the police have considerable discretionary power. Had I one statement, one witness, one instance, in contradiction of Mr.

VanBrunt's guilt, I should certainly deliver him from this place. I have the authority to release him, or can come by it, but I must have the justification."

"Then let us get justification," said Poe. "Let us go and speak with our only witness. It should not be difficult to locate a boy who has the misfortune to have a clubfoot."

# Chapter 6

## A WITNESS SPEAKS

It was nearing dusk as we approached Paradise Square. It had been raining a cold rain on and off all day. For the moment it had let up, but the ground was spongy and the morning's laundry, hanging about the fence of Paradise Square and creating the mirage of an Arabian tent from a distance and in the weak shadowed light, was still wet, and, on closer inspection, covered with a film of black soot from nearby stacks and street fires. The washerwomen would wait for it to dry in the first sun and simply shake what soot they could out of it. Especially in winter, the locals often looked smeared and streaked.

"There's the boy," I said, needlessly pointing him out. Older than the other boys, bigger, and clubfooted, he was not easy to miss.

"I know that boy," said Poe. "He was at the Old Brewery—sleeping in the room where you found me. I didn't notice his foot. Introduce us, Sergeant. Give me official color, if you will, so that I can ask my questions freely, with apparent authority."

Poe and Mullins hung back a few yards while I stepped up to the Gimp. I told the boy that Poe was a police inspector and that he must answer his questions with great honesty or fear for the consequences.

"He ain't no copper," said the boy, sneeringly. "I seed him drunk last night at the Brewery'."

"He was engaged in dangerous secret work, you little rogue. Come along now."

The clubfooted boy and the noseless man eyed each other with distaste. Poe took the boy's shoulder in his hand to shift his attention from the ivory nose. For his part, Mullins had eyed the boy as if he were looking at a grotesque. I had observed before that these toughs were sensitive enough about themselves but insensitive to the point of brutality about one another.

The Gimp was dressed in ragged garments and mud-spattered boots. One boot, built up in the sole and heel was twisted nearly backwards. He had shrewd, evasive eyes, but spoke directly when asked what he had seen and heard on the evening of the murder. I was struck by his alacrity. These boys did not rap with "coppers."

"We was guardin' the laundry," he said, hefting an omnipresent brick-bat. "Then we got into a game of craps. It was gettin' dark. We was gaddered by the east gate, so we would take turns to stand guard by the west gate, and that's where I was when I seed this Hot Corn Goil go into the park. In a minute she screamt. I looks in the gate. This gent is bent down over her and he's got this meat cleaver in his hand. He's kilt her. Then comes a crowd, and the cove can't get away. But he don't even try. He just stares around at everybody like he's crazy or sumpin'."

"What then?" said Poe.

"Well, the leadderhead comes."

"And then?" prompted Poe.

"And then you ast me the same questions that the leadder-head who stayed in the park ast me—and now I gotter answer the same questions again. Maybe I shouldn't have squealt."

"Why did you?" asked Poe.

"Cuz I couldn't run. Lookit me foot."

"You could have stayed and said nothing. Everyone else did."

"They'd of beat it outter me."

"How did the patrolman know you knew anything until you volunteered it?"

The boy shrugged. "Just the same," he said.

"No, not just the same," said Poe. "But no matter. Let's have a look inside the fence."

We stepped into the park by the west gate.

"It's only a few square yards of mud," said Poe. "No need to ask where the body was found. Where is the body now?"

"The pauper's graveyard, I should think, sir."

"Sergeant, it's been a long afternoon. I feel the need of some refreshment. Let's get off the streets for a bit and do some thinking. There's a diving bell across the way. I suggest we adjourn to it. But first, would you please spread the word among the boys now guarding the laundry that I will give a substantial reward for any information about the murder. They can call on me at my table in the aforementioned establishment at their leisure for the next hour. I'm sure that such clever young coves will be able to find an anonymous method of approach."

It occurred to me that I should have to pay any reward. "What good will it do, Mr. Poe?" I asked. "They're a bunch of little liars and will say anything for money—anything but the truth. You might interview one who was not even there Monday night, and yet he'll tell you that he saw every-thing."

"Let's try it, shall we?" said Poe, and walked off toward the rum parlor. Mullins stood in doubt for a moment, then fol-lowed in Poe's wake leaving the clubfooted boy with a last vision of the "bloke with no boke," as he would undoubtedly later describe the mutilated Mullins.

"Is that all?" he asked.

"For now," I said, and went about my business among the other boys, who had hung back, apparently in fear and def-erence to the Gimp, but whose curious eyes, buried in uncut hair, so that they almost seemed in the backs of their heads, had never left us.

# Chapter 7

## DIVIDED JUDGMENT

In a quarter of an hour I found Poe and Mullins in the diving bell. They were drinking rum in silence. The place smelled of sooty air and rising damp, of wet, dirty clothing, alcohol and tobacco fumes. Poe appeared oblivious of this rank olla podrida. He sipped a rum, his dark eyebrows down in a V, deep in thought. I wasn't certain that he was aware of me.

"You did not like the Gimp," I said to Mullins as I sat down.

"Didn't like, didn't dislike," said Mullins. "His foot was ugly."

"Mr. Mullins has a sense of beauty," Poe said. "But it's un-cultivated, or he'd know that to clothe misfortune with com-passion is to see it as poignancy." He paused. "But the boy is lying, of course, not so much in what he has said, but in what he has not said. Think about it. It's totally outside of his character to volunteer information to the police. Then why should he do it? He's protecting someone, perhaps un-der compulsion, or perhaps for reward. Who? The murderer, most probably. So, he leaves the murderer out of his story. Does that make sense to you, Sergeant?"

"It's possible."

"Yes, *possible*. It's quickly formulated. I've thought of it almost as I've said it. Sergeant, go back and get the Gimp and bring him to me. I think we can get to the bottom of this almost immediately."

"How, Mr. Poe?"

"I have a method for getting at the truth which few can resist."

"I'll get the ugly little beggar," said Mullins, and went off after the Gimp.

"If you can get the truth out of that hardcase, Mr. Poe," I said, "you're a better man than I am."

"It's clear that you're too humane a person to attempt to employ force upon a child, though not all your colleagues, I'm certain, would be so scrupulous. I, however, have no need of force. My only bludgeon will be the gentle tick-tock of the pocket watch that hangs by your waistband chain. Let me see it, if you will."

I gave him my watch, which he took by the chain and swung above his glass. The watch caught the dancing candlelight and glittered as it swung.

"There is just the right amount of light," he said.

"The right amount of light for what, sir? Look here, you're not going to try to bribe him to the truth with my gold watch, are you? Because it was a gift from my late father—"

"No, no, Sergeant. "I wouldn't offer another man's watch away, nor my own in a bribe. Have you heard of mesmerism?"

27

"I can't say that I have, sir." Indeed, it was the first that I had heard of the hypnotic science, or art, but have read much about it since. At the time I thought: now we shall see what special powers this man has above those of an average intelligent man like myself. At that moment, I realized that my vanity secretly hoped that Poe would fail in his purpose, while my better nature was of course wishing for his success. I was ashamed to realize that I was not quite single-minded. I hadn't yet decided how I felt about Edgar Allen Poe. His work, of which I had read a good deal, had my highest admiration. My judgment of the man hung fire.

Mullins returned without the Gimp. "Funny-foot's nowhere to be found," he said.

"Damn!" whispered Poe.

Just then a street urchin stepped up to our table, smoking a cigar—-a cherub of a boy, about ten, with a heart-shaped, pug-nosed face, and a wild mass of dirty golden curls. "My name's Danny" said he. "What's the reward for my story?"

## Chapter 8

## HYPNOTIZED TO TIME

Poe looked at me with eyebrows a third of the way up his enormous forehead. He said: "Sit down, boy, and take that cigar out of your mouth." He pushed a chair toward the child. To me he said: "Either he knows something or he doesn't. In any case, we shall soon see."

He held my watch by the chain and began swinging it in a slow arc near the candle, so that a small breeze caused a slight fluttering of the flame.

"This watch, Danny—it *was* Danny, wasn't it?"

"Yes, sir. My name's Danny Devlin."

"This watch, Danny, is very valuable. It's made of gold—do you see?"

"Yes, sir—"

"Beautiful, isn't it, Danny?"

"Worth somewhat, sir—"

"Watch it swing, Danny. Look how it glitters when it swings. It makes you sleepy, Danny, doesn't it?"

With a few passes he had the boy in his power.

29

He led with a few general questions, such as would the boy be truthful, to which the boy replied that he would, and did the boy know anything of what had happened on the night of the murder, to which the boy replied that he did.

Poe glanced at me. "He was there, and he'll tell us the truth as he knows it."

"It's like the Devil has come above," said Mullins, who seemed as entranced by Poe as the boy did.

"It's not black magic," said Poe. "It's merely science in action. Now," he said to the boy, "tell us about Monday night."

"Me . . . and the Gimp," the boy began, slowly, "and a few others was guardin' the laundry. Then we started a game of dice. We had the game by the east gate, so we was takin' turns—one at a time—goin' to watch at the west gate. With the laundry up you can't see nothin' through the fence— somebody got to be over there. It was the Gimp's turn to stand guard on the west side. He went over there. Some of us shootin' craps had our backs to the east gate, but I was lookin' that way. It was about dark, and I saw that gent, the one they arrested, coming kind of wobberly toward the Square. He was pretty close to us, and then we heard a horrible scream. It was a woman's voice. The man began to run towards the park, towards the gate. He ran in and when we looked he was holdin' the girl. She was dead, bloody—"

"Danny," said Poe, "you say that you heard the scream before the man entered the park?"

30

"Yeah. When he heard the scream he began to run."

"He heard the scream," said Poe, "and ran *into* the park?"

"Yes, sir."

Poe looked at me. That was it. VanBrunt had not misplaced his confidence in Poe.

"You said, Sergeant, that you only needed a contradiction to the Gimp's testimony to justify VanBrunt's release. Here you have it. The girl was attacked before VanBrunt entered the Square. It's not conclusive. The boy might be mistaken as to the sequence of events. But so might the Gimp, though I think his version is a lie by omission. The girl might have screamed for some other reason, a minor attack previous to VanBrunt's, it could be argued. But, in light of his avowed intention to propose marriage, witnessed by, among others, our friend Mullins here, that's unlikely. I think you now have what you need to justify VanBrunt's immediate release."

"Mr. Poe," I said, "can you make this boy repeat his story at any time you desire to hear it."

"I can. And furthermore, if we can find the Gimp, I can get the truth out of him. He would know the name of—or, at least, be able to describe—the murderer, for I have come to think that no one else but the murderer would have reason to have him lie."

"It's the Devil's work, Mr. Poe, that you be about."

"Not at all, Mr. Mullins. It's a scientific principle at work, one rediscovered in the latter times by Anton Mesmer, a person of doubtful morality but acute observation. Would you like me to mesmerize you?"

"Ye gads, *no!*" cried Mullins. Poe laughed, and turned his attention to the boy.

"Danny?"

"Yes, sir?"

"I am going to count to three and snap my fingers, and when I do you'll feel perfectly normal."

"Yes, sir."

"*One.* Mr. Mullins, would you please go up to the bar and get us a round of drinks. This concentration, combined with my somewhat weakened condition, has given me a head-ache. *Two.*"

Mullins left the table looking backward over his shoulder as if at a coven of witches.

"Danny," Poe said, "we shall want to see you again. I want you to come every morning to watch the laundry—say at about ten o'clock—do you understand?"

"Yes, sir."

"*Three.*" Poe snapped his fingers. The boy looked at him, shook his head slightly, and said: "It wasn't a man, you see, sir, it was an ape that done it. Do you want me to tell you how it happened?"

"No, boy," said Poe. "But the sergeant here has a penny for you."

I gave the boy a penny and watched him as he left. He was quite confused.

When Mullins returned with our drinks, I saluted the writer in the name of VanBrunt.

# Chapter 9

## A REPRIEVE

At Red Kate's table, Poe was flanked by Mullins and Max Fisch. The latter was well known to me. I had had occasion to arrest little Max, a screwsman, a burglar who uses skeleton keys or lockpicks. He was a pathetic fellow who suffered from a type of nervous disorder which caused a constant trembling, sometimes shaking, of his long-nailed claw like hands. This affliction must have caused him much trouble on the job. Max was a notorious coward, of the cornered-rat variety.

Mullins, Fisch, and Poe were drinking rum. I gave Poe a keen look. He seemed in command of himself, though there was a bit of the glass in his eye.

VanBrunt and I sat down.

"Eddie," said VanBrunt, "I knew if anyone could do it, you could, but I never imagined you could do it this quickly, and that I should be free tonight."

"They say Eddie's a genius," said Kate.

"He's Nicky," said Mullins.

Poe looked at me.

"The Devil," I translated.

Poe smiled. "You must thank Sergeant Goode for your release, Peter. I was merely able to put things in balance."

"Sir, I'm an ordinary patrolman. I work according to the principles I know, but what you were able to do—"

"Not at all. Despite your numerous disclaimers, you're an excellent policeman, and a highly intelligent one. Furthermore, I should like to report that I am neither the Devil nor C. Auguste Dupin, my fictional detective, but merely a writer, to be rated by others, with a certain, as it were, storehouse of quaint and curious lore, some bit of which, here or there, may prove useful. But let me remind everyone that, though we have obtained Peter's freedom, we have not entirely cleared him of a charge of murder, which hoped-for end can only be attained, in my view, by the discovery of the true murderer."

"He can cast a spell on people," said Mullins, "and make them say anything he wants. How do we know what they say is the truth?"

"That's a fair question," said Poe. "But not to the point. First, get what might be the truth, any way you can, then confirm it. Half the battle is in the knowing. I'm certain that Sergeant Goode can find a method of having the truth speak for itself—which is to say, of having Danny Devlin repeat his story out of my influence."

"How do you do it, Eddie?" asked Kate.

"It's mesmerism, isn't it?" asked VanBrunt. "Sergeant Goode told me what you did. How long have you been practicing it, Eddie?"

"Animal magnetism, more lately called mesmerism, has been an interest of mine for some years. My goal is to employ it as a means of strengthening the will in the dying, so that they are able to hold back the encroachment of death beyond the capacity of the body—which is to say, ultimately, to cause the dead to remain quick."

"Black magic!" cried Mullins.

Poe laughed. "No, no—I said that for your benefit, Mr. Mullins. What interests me in mesmerism has nothing to do with the black arts. It's science—and science, indeed put to the service of humanity. I myself can eliminate pain in some circumstances. But there are few today in the medical profession who will listen when you speak of mesmerism—due to the charlatanism of some of its early practitioners. And, I might add—especially for your benefit, Mr. Mullins—due as well to the superstitions of earlier times. Yet no words are so true as 'This too will pass.' I conceive the day when teeth will be extracted painlessly from the jaws of mesmerized subjects; and when police officers, such as yourself, Sergeant, will use this science as a tool for getting at the truth, as you've seen demonstrated today—as I'll demonstrate now, if one of you will consent to be my subject."

"None of that witchcraft with me!" cried Mullins. He had a manifest awe, even fear, of Poe.

"It has been my observation that the untutored are filled with baseless fears, which allow for their manipulation by the unscrupulous," I directed at Poe.

"L'Imagination fait tout," Poe said; "le magnétisme nul."

"Fishy, you be the subject," said Kate.

"Not me," said Max Fisch, waving away the idea. "I don't like nothin' I don't understand."

"You'll do it," said Kate, "or I'll have both your Jack Cove ears in that bottle behind the bar."

"You'd not have my ears, Kate!" Fisch sank low in his chair, his hands repeatingly clapping his reddening ears.

"I've had better men's, and spit them from these red lips."

"Do what Kate says," ordered Mullins.

"I assure you," said Poe, "I'll do you no harm. Your watch, Sergeant. Now, quiet, please!"

Within moments Poe had the timorous man in his power.

"How does it work now?" asked Kate.

"Give me a question to ask of him."

"Ask him," said Kate, "if he's a fool."

"Are you a fool?" asked Poe.

"No, sir," said Max Fisch.

"But he is!" cried Kate.

"But he doesn't think he is," said Poe.

"Then the more fool he," said Kate.

"The more fool all of us," said Poe, and gave me a charming wink.

"Ask him," said VanBrunt, "if he knew Mary Hart."

"Ah," sighed Poe, and repeated the question to Max Fisch.

"I knowed her. A bleak mort."

"A pretty girl," I translated.

"Ask him," said VanBrunt, "if he loved her."

"My friend," said Poe, "you're pursuing a morbid line of questioning."

"No," said VanBrunt, "you mistake me. I merely wish you to know that all who knew her came to love her, as I've told you."

"In that case," said Poe, and asked the question.

"Yes, sir," answered Max Fisch. "I loved her. She were beautiful."

"Would you kill for her?" asked VanBrunt.

"Answer," said Poe, his face disturbed.

"I would if I was made to."

I didn't like the cast of things, and said so.

"You're quite right, Sergeant," said Poe, and snapped his fingers to awaken Max Fisch.

"What happened," said Fisch.

"Nothing," said Kate, frowning.

"Will you consent to be my subject?" Poe asked Kate.

"What, me?"

"Are you afraid?" asked Fisch. "It don't hurt none. It's like it didn't even happen. It did happen, didn't it?"

"It did," said VanBrunt.

"I'll not have anyone in control of me," said Kate. "That's out!"

"She don't got to," seconded Mullins.

Poe rose from his chair. "I'm going to retire," he said, and placing a hand on VanBrunt's thin shoulder, he added, "I can rest now that I know my dear friend is at liberty." He then turned his gaze to Kate and said, "Do you mind if I take this bottle with me?"

"Take it," she said. "You're my guest for as long as you wish."

Her interest shifted to VanBrunt. She put an arm over his shoulder and kissed him on the forehead. "Me foolish old buck," she said, "welcome home."

I bid them good night, and followed Poe to our rooms on the second floor. Outside his door, he turned to me and said:

"Has it occurred to you that Red Kate might have killed Mary Hart?"

"Not until now," I said.

"Tell me," he said. "You know her. Is she capable of murder?"

"Indeed," said I. "She's probably dispatched a few."

"Jealousy is a powerful motive, Sergeant."

"Yes, sir—it is."

Poe opened his door.

"Sergeant."

"Yes, sir?"

"I should be careful of burglars. Many must have observed your gold watch."

"When I stay in a place like this, Mr. Poe, I make a man-sized mound of my belongings and the bed-clothes and such and put it under the blanket. Then I stretch out under the bed, my pistol at the ready."

"A tactic worthy of emulation. I have no pistol, but I have my bottle of rum."

"These clapboard buildings are tinderboxes, Mr. Poe. I should be careful not to drink so much that I might sleep through a fire alarm. Just in case, sir, there's a door to an outside stairway at the end of the hall."

"I see it, Sergeant. But don't worry. I'm a light sleeper."

"Goodnight, Mr. Poe."

# Chapter 10

## POE IS MURDERED

Twinges of conscience had troubled me from the onset of this investigation. First, I knew myself to be a dupe, chosen for my inexperience, for nothing else could explain my sudden rise in rank, from an ordinary leatherhead to a detective, and I felt keenly the dishonor underlying the situation, though I did not understand its nature, the what and why of it. Then I had clutched at a straw, when VanBrunt suggested bringing Edgar Poe in. This was hope for myself as well as VanBrunt, and I had pursued the idea and the poet with vigor. His reputation at what he had called "ratiocination" was great. Many eminent people had thought he had hit upon the solution to the Mary Rogers murder case, a real New York crime, in his tale "The Mystery of Marie Roget," set in Paris, France. He wrote brilliantly of crime and detection—who better to have on our side? But now, as I set up my false sleeping body on top of the small sunken bed and spread the moth-eaten blanket over it, I thought of the true nature of the situation.

Poe was a fine writer, perhaps a great one, given time, but he was not an actual detective, and the fear overcame me that I might have placed such a man in a dangerous situation. What would the world think of me if I were, even inadvertently responsible for his death? I slid under the bed and held my pistol at the ready. Now that I thought back on the day, I realized that it was Poe who had kept us here at Red Kate's. Why? Did he like the atmosphere, or did he have something else in mind? I had observed from time to time during the course of the day, a certain bulldog tenacity in the set of jaw and a kind of zealotry in his large, burning eyes. He was definitely not a timid man. The thought occurred to me that he was greatly interested in the situation. Perhaps he thought of Mary Hart's murder as potential material for his writing. It occurred to me for the first time that I might turn up as a character in one of his tales. He seemed to like me well enough, but what he really thought—well. I even had the temerity to dream that I might someday write a memoir about him and this—my first—case. I had dozed off. Had Poe come into the room, or had I dreamed it? Had someone shot him? I was shaken, and got out from under the bed and stood in the dark room, wondering what was real and what I had dreamed.

I stepped into the hall, pistol in hand. Poe was standing at his door, holding a pistol, his usually pale face ashen.

"What happened?" I asked.

"Someone," he said calmly, "has murdered me."

"Are you shot?" I asked excitedly. I looked him over but could see no blood.

"My other self," he said, pointing into the room. He had made a mound of his coat, pillow, and bedclothes, as I had. "If you will look closely," he said, "you'll see that I have been shot through the heart."

Red Kate and Mullins had arrived at the top of the stairs. We could look from the balcony down into the *Ballum-rancum* below, as the mob who were the celebrants of the ball could look up at us. Morning, noon, or night, the party was never over at the Emerald Isle. One could read on the faces in the mob the annoyance felt at the interruption of the festivities. The general question appeared to be: Should they dive for cover or carry on?

Kate stopped in her flight and called down to them that everything was under control, to go on about their business. She and Mullins came up to us.

"What happened?" she asked.

"Somebody tried to kill Mr. Poe," I told her.

"With this," said Poe, hefting the pistol like a man who knew weapons. "I was sleeping, the shot rang out, the door was slammed. Fortunately, I was sleeping under the bed and not in it."

"Under the bed?" said Kate. "What kind of place do you think I operate here?"

"But, madam," said Poe, "you compel me to embarrass myself in order to avoid any insult to you or to your establishment. I was sleeping under the bed," he whispered, "because that was where the consumption of your marvelous rum had driven me. But the pile of my clothes on the bed must have seemed the shape of a man—they do look so, do they not?—to the rogue who shot at them. It was a thief, no doubt. It happens in the best of places. I think I must have groaned or made a noise—perhaps I kicked in my sleep— and startled him, and in a reflex action he shot?"

"Why do you say that?" I asked. "Perhaps he—or *she*," I added pointedly—*intended* to kill you."

"I should think not," said Poe, "for the reason that an assassin who has calculated his assassination does not drop his weapon in departure. I stubbed my toe on this at the door. See, it smells of the shot."

"Look," said Kate. "The initials carved on the wooden handles, both sides—*M.F.* That's Max Fisch's pistol. I should know, as he's hocked it with me these many times. Nobody burgles in my place. I'll kill him!"

"He must have thought that gold watch belonged to you, Mr. Poe," said Mullins. "You seed how his hands shake. The gun must have popped right out of his grip."

I wondered aloud that Max Fisch should try his business with Poe; for he, like Mullins, viewed Poe as being almost supernatural. "Greed would not overcome such fear," I said.

"Perhaps not," said Poe thoughtfully. "But enough fear can make a man act the shadow of a hero. I should like to ask Fisch about all this."

"He's gone," said Mullins. "Him and Mr. VanBrunt left together."

"Left?" Poe looked upset, a condition which VanBrunt's absence caused me to share with him. Poe tilted his head, and it was as though you could see his mind working. "What time is it, Sergeant?"

I consulted my watch. "Five in the morning, sir."

45

"Where did Mr. VanBrunt intend to go?" Poe asked. "Do you have any idea?"

"Yes, sir," said Mullins. "Him and Max Fisch was talking, and he—he was pretty drunk—he said that he wanted to talk to that Gimp boy who spoke against him. Max Fisch said he'd show him where to find the boy. Max Fisch was drunk, too, sir. I expect they are wandering around in the streets."

"Why didn't you stop him?" I asked. "Or stay with him?"

"I have me own work to do for Miss Kate. I got to control that mob down there, that they don't break nothing or each other—it's me job. I ain't no wet-nurse."

"I think we had better find VanBrunt," Poe said.

"Yes, before he gets his throat cut," said Kate. "You go with them, No-Nose. See that everybody's safe."

"Do you think he'll be at the Old Brewery?" I asked.

"That's where the Gimp probably is," said Poe. "It's the logical place to look."

"We dressed and made our way through the Five Points. Mullins' giant form and frightening face assured us of safe conduct, though the denizens of the hellish place were on the prowl about us. It took only a few minutes to get from Kate's to the Old Brewery.

Upon entering the room in which I had first found Poe, we found VanBrunt apparently in a drunken sleep at the same

46

table. I shook him, but he could not be immediately awakened. Poe went over to the Gimp, and in a moment called me over.

"He's been strangled," Poe said. "The miserable end of a miserable life."

"The poor wretch!" I said. "Did VanBrunt do it? Have we been wrong?"

"Let's not leap to conclusions. Where's Max Fisch?"

"I don't know," I said, "but I think we'd better get these two out of here first. We can do nothing here anyway. If I bring in the Municipals, we'll have a riot on our hands. The department's not strong enough to deal with that. Mullins," I ordered, "take the boy's body, wrap it in the blanket, and bring it. Mr. Poe, let's you and I get VanBrunt out of here." We hauled his inert body to its feet, threw its limp arms over our shoulders, and proceeded apace. "Mr. Poe . . . Eddie . . . I am worried about you," I confided. "Nay, sir, I am frightened for your life. I shouldn't have heeded VanBrunt and brought you into this horror."

Poe laughed. "You may have forgotten, Sergeant, but horror is my business. There is a movement of larger shadows behind the puppets we observe. Someone who has been physically close to us is responsible for the shooting in my room, someone in the immediate grouping of puppets before us, but it little relevancy bears. I am concerned with the puppeteers, the string-pullers who hide backstage. We shall find them out, Sergeant, have no fear."

We encountered no one on our way out; but, had we, I doubt that it would have mattered. To the denizens of the Old Brewery, it would not have signified to see two men carrying between them a comatose third, nor the body of a boy in the arms of an ivory-nosed brute.

# Chapter 11

## NOISE OF NIAGARA

Over toward the east a whisper of light could almost be heard, like lace curtains slowly drawn back. Soon the sky-line with its sails and masts, punctuated by church spires, would stand in ever more defined silhouette. "Mullins," I called to the striding giant, "when we get VanBrunt and the Gimp's body to the hospital, I want you to come back and find Max Fisch. Bring him to Red Kate's. Lock him in a room if you must."

"Yes, sir," Mullins said, and vanished into the smoky dark ahead of us.

"Note," said Poe, "how he can carry the body of the boy under one arm and still out stride a racehorse."

Near Paradise Square we heard the clomping of a cab horse coming in our direction and hailed it. Apparently the driver was reluctant to stop in the dark middle of the slum. He whipped the horses on. I let Poe take VanBrunt's full weight, and seized the nearer horse by its bridle, letting him feel my weight. When I had slowed its progress, I flashed my copper star up at the driver. We got VanBrunt and ourselves aboard and ordered the driver to take us to the City Hospital, "On the gallop!"

"As far as we know," I said to Poe, "Max Fisch was the last person to be in the company of Mr. VanBrunt—excepting,

49

perhaps, the Gimp—and I'm anxious to hear what he has to say. More, there's the attempt on you. We must bring him to book for that, in any case."

"I doubt very much if Max Fisch had anything to do with the shot fired at me," said Poe.

"Do you suppose Mullins will turn up at the hospital?"

"He'll probably beat us there. His legs are longer and probably more powerful than the legs of these old drays." Poe looked worried. "There's something more wrong with our friend here than mere inebriation," he said. "His sleep is too deep. I fear that the alcohol has affected his brain. He's comatose."

"Perhaps he's hurt himself otherwise," I said.

"I see no abrasions."

"The hospital isn't far. Just up on Broadway."

"I hope that you haven't lost faith in the innocence of our friend here," said Poe.

"I have not, sir. Oh, there was the shadow of a doubt back there. Just for a moment. But when I undertook to release him, I put myself at risk, and, if I let him remain at liberty in these circumstances, I'll look a fool."

"Does that mean that you intend to place him under arrest again?"

"I'll consider him in my custody for now. As, indeed, he still is, in any case."

"Do you share my feeling," said Poe, "that the other boy, Devlin, may be in danger? If the Gimp was killed because his testimony was false, and the truth might have come out had he lived, Devlin may also be in danger because his testimony is true, and would tend to clear VanBrunt. The Gimp's murder was an attempt to make VanBrunt look guilty—that is, the murder of the main witness against him. But, if that's the case, it follows that the main witness in his favor could also be in jeopardy."

"Yes," I said. "I see that. We'd better pick the boy up."

"And keep him with us," said Poe. "When I mesmerized him, I suggested that he go to Paradise Square every morning at ten o'clock. It's his habit to do so anyway. I had simply to reinforce it. I thought a time might be at hand when we'd want to get hold of him. I'm certain that we'll be able to find him at Paradise Square at ten. It would be so much more convenient, would it not, if these boys had homes?"

"Their wretched lives are our disgrace," I said.

"If we must wait until ten," said Poe, "to see the boy, why not put the intervening hours to good use?"

"What do you suggest?"

"I'd like to interview Mary Hart's mother."

51

When we reined in at the hospital, the doctor on duty was waiting at the door. "You must be the policeman with the injured man," he said. "A giant with an ivory nose came rushing in here minutes ago and dumped a body in my lap. I tried to hold him, but had little chance of success. He said you were right behind him."

We went inside and the doctor made a quick examination of VanBrunt. The Gimp's body lay on a nearby table. "What is it?" Poe asked the doctor impatiently. "Is it the drink?"

"I think not," said the doctor. "Feel here, at the back of his head."

"What is it?" I asked, as Poe probed VanBrunt's head.

"A soft spot."

"A swelling," said the doctor. "The skin isn't broken, so I should say that this man is suffering from a concussion, brought about by being hit with a blackjack. We see it all the time here."

"What's to be done?" I asked. "Will he be all right?"

"Chances are good," said the doctor, "that he'll come out of it, but it could be hours, even days."

"You'll see to the boy?"

"Any family?"

"None known to us."

"We'll see to the body. Another pauper, poor kid."

Outside, on the stone steps of the hospital, facing Broadway, we paused for a breath of cold morning air. The daybreak traffic of heavily laden carts and wagons, along with innumerable omnibuses, passed before us.

"I'd like a cup of strong, hot coffee," Poe said.

"I know a good cheap restaurant—the Stage Door—across the alley from the stage door of the Phoenix Theatre."

As we walked down Broadway, Poe said, in an uncharacteristically loud voice, speaking above the roar of iron wheels on granite that someone once likened to "the sound of Niagara heard from the Cataract Hotel"—"Just look at this, Sergeant." He waved a hand at the spectacle. "Here we are at the center of the wealth and commerce of the greatest state in these United States. When the carriage trade appears later today, Broadway will be filled with carriages conveying occupants whose rich haberdashery will display a contempt for money. Let's say, the VanBrunts. They'll step down from their carriages, aided by footmen, and visit some of the most elegant stores in the world. At Tiffany's they might purchase a bauble that would keep a family alive for a year. At J. & C. Berrien they might spend Fifteen Thousand Dollars for a roomful of furniture. And no Blind Tiger whiskey for such gentry. They'll buy champagne at John Duncan & Son. The books that I need and cannot afford, they'll think nothing of purchasing as gifts for their semi-literate brethren. And this very Sunday they'll congregate before yon Trinity Church with its spire aimed at heaven and its doors opened to Wall Street. This is the glory of progress. But what of poverty? Do they ever look at it? I'd like to go out into the middle of Broadway and wave their carriages but one minute's jostle down Anthony Street to the Five Points and Paradise Square so that they could have a look at the source of their happiness; the misery they feed upon."

# Chapter 12

## THE PHOENIX IN FLAME

Phoenix Alley was a long, curving, cobbled alley lined with small shops. We turned into it, and when we had walked about half its length, we became aware of a thin, dark fog.

"Fire ahead!" I cried.

Now we could see plumes of smoke.

"It's the theatre," I said. "We must sound the alarm!"

But immediately we heard the alarm bells.

There was a great deal of anguished pounding at the inside of the stage door. Poe and I tried to open it, but it was locked, or jammed. We gave up, and ran the few yards out of the alley to the front of the theatre, where we were greeted by the sight of a giant on a barrel fighting off other giants by making wide, ruthless swings with a seven-foot hickory staff that dangled a dead rabbit at its end.

"The hydrant is under the barrel," I told Poe. "The thug is saving it for his fire company. He's a Dead Rabbit. The others look like Bowery Boys."

"But there are people trapped in that theatre, and these fools are playing at who's first!"

I reached out to stop him, but he strode beyond my grasp. He went up behind the Dead Rabbit, caught the staff at its end in a back-swing, jerked it from the hands of the surprised volunteer fireman, whirled it above his own head, and fairly batted the Dead Rabbit from the barrel as if he were a ball in a game of rounders. Immediately, the opposing volunteer firemen, the Bowery Boys, sent up a great cheer, and fell to removing the barrel from the hydrant, the wooden fire-plug from the log-pipe, and hooking up their hose.

Poe ran to the glassed front doors of the theatre and smashed them with the staff.

Three coughing actors emerged in a puff of smoke.

"Kevin!" I cried.

One of the actors was an acquaintance of mine. Kevin O'Connell, the comic-actor, who lived down the hall from me at my boarding house in Greenwich Village.

Kevin threw his arms around me, gasping. I held him steady until he caught his breath. Then he cried, "That divil of a gangster would have let us die before he'd let the Dead Rabbits be beaten to a fire by the Bowery Boys. I thank your friend heartily for saving my life."

Poe looked perplexed. "Gangster? I thought he was a mad fireman."

"These volunteer firemen are all members of gangs," I said.

"Well, not all," Kevin corrected. I remembered now that he had been one.

"Most," I modified.

Kevin said: "The divils fight each other with brickbats and guns when there's no fire to fight, and then they fight each other for the right to fight the fire!"

We retired to the Stage Door Restaurant to have coffee, and to watch through the window as the fire was fought.

"I knew you were working at the Phoenix, Kevin," I said, "but what were you doing there at this early hour?"

"Rehearsing a trick. We've been at it all night. I think one of us got tired and fell asleep with a cigar in his teeth. Oh, it's been an *awful* night! We were doing a business with a series of trap doors, and we couldn't get the damned things to work."

"I especially dislike a theatre burning," said Poe. "My parents were actors."

"Were they, now?"

"My mother has played that very theatre. You may have heard of her—Elizabeth Arnold Poe?"

"Poe? Are you, by chance, the writer, Poe?"

"He is," I said, feeling a certain pride in the fellowship of such a well-known figure.

"I've read your work, Mr. Poe," said Kevin.

"I hope you enjoyed it."

"Oh, indeed! Particularly 'The Raven.' Why, it must be the most famous poem in the world! I don't know how anyone can write like that."

It was strange to think that this shabby man who sat sipping black, steaming coffee at the table with me should be the author of, as Kevin had put it, "the most famous poem in the world."

"It's down to smoldering smoke," said Poe.

"Let's go and have a look," said Kevin.

The firemen had smashed in the stage door.

We made our way through the still steaming debris and walked out on the stage. Morning sun glared down on us through great, jagged holes in walls and ceiling. Blue sky and white clouds peppered with ashes, drifted, plain to be seen, above us.

Kevin showed us the traps upon which he had been working, a series of three, each a square yard, nine feet across the stage.

"You see," said he, "I run ahead of my pursuer, somebody pulls the traps just as I cross them, and down goes my enemy. Down there are straw mattresses to break the fall."

"A beam has dropped from the ceiling, through the traps," said Poe, "and ignited the mattresses. They're gone. You see?"

Indeed, there were no mattresses.

"'Twould be a breakneck fall without 'em," said Kevin.

"How do the traps work?" asked Poe.

"Over here, these levers."

Kevin moved the levers into position. The doors sprung.

"Now, you see? Look at that! Now I've got working traps and no theatre. Can you beat it! And they talk of the luck of the Irish!"

# Chapter 13

## SPEAK OF THE DEAD

The leatherhead who had arrested VanBrunt had supplied me with Mrs. Hart's address, a tenement on Ann Street. He had instructed me to tap on the window, first floor front.

VanBrunt had never met Mrs. Hart, but Mary had told him that her mother was blind. Only yellowed whites showed in the slits of her shrunken eyes. Her hair was yellowed grey like her winkled, careworn face. She hugged a Bible to her bosom, and leaned on a cane. I explained our errand and she admitted us, leading us through a musty hall, into a sparsely furnished room, and made her way to a center table. She offered us each a chair and a cup of tea. The footboard of a bed peeked modestly from behind a screen. A larger Bible rested on a stand near the table. Though I had trouble adjusting my eyes to the dismal light, I saw that it was open to "The Revelations of Jesus Christ."

Mrs. Hart apologized at having no biscuits to offer us. "I have no income now. Mary was my sole support. The ladies of the mission have been taking care of me since her death. But I don't know how long they'll be willing to do so. They've spoken of an institution that takes care of such as myself, poor, blind and useless."

"Never useless, madam," said Poe. He sipped his steaming tea.

"How can I be of help?"

"You can tell us about Mary's friends," I said.

"Mary wasn't a girl for making friends. She kept to herself. She hated the life down here and tried to stay apart from it. But she did tell me about Mr. VanBrunt. Really, except when working, she saw no one at all—until him. But she was in love with him, and from what she told me about him, I believe he loved her. It was Mary's intention to accept him in marriage, if he proposed."

"Then you are not aware that she had any other friends?" I asked.

"Perhaps one of the other Hot Corn Girls, but I know of no one specifically. When she wasn't working she stayed home with me and cooked and cleaned and did chores about the house. She read a great deal. After working all night, she'd come home early in the morning and read to me from the big Bible there. On Sundays, the only day I venture out, she took me to services at the mission. Oh," she said, hugging the small Bible closer to her breast, "you must be wondering about this one. I mean, because of my blindness. I can't read it, of course, but I never have it out of reach. Holding it is like holding the past. My other daughter, Lucy, gave me it. But it hasn't been opened since Lucy's death. She made me promise that no one but herself would read to me from it. And no one has. But please forgive me for chattering on. When one is lonely one talks at the drop of a hat, about everything and anything."

Poe said: "Did you approve of Mr. VanBrunt?"

"Oh, yes—from what Mary told me."

"Then you doubt his guilt?"

"I *know* he didn't kill Mary."

"How do you know that?" I asked.

"Because I know who killed her."

"Who?" I asked.

"The Butcher's Gang."

Poe was still, studying the blind face.

"Boss Mead's boys? What makes you say that?" I asked.

"Because they did the same to my other daughter, Lucy."

"The Butcher's Gang," said Mrs. Hart, "is a gang that's part of the Plug Uglies, and—"

"Excuse me for a moment, madam," said Poe. "Sergeant, are you familiar with this gang?"

"Yes, sir," I said. "The Five Points is full of gangs—the Forty Thieves, the Roach Guards, the Dead Rabbits—like the one you batted from the barrel—the Chichesters, the Shirt Tails, and so on. Some of these gangs began as social clubs, and evolved into volunteer fire companies. Some have become political and criminal organizations. I think I told you that Boss Meade began as a butcher. I'm a greenhorn, as Red Kate said, so no expert, but years ago, from what I gather, Meade started a social club made up of butchers, which eventually joined ranks with the Plug Uglies, a very large gang, numbering into the hundreds. The Plug Uglies are a strong part of Meade's constituency. They are also the Red Dragons Hook & Ladder Company, of which Meade is chief."

"That's right, said Mrs. Hart. "The Butcher's Gang is part of the Plug Uglies, and my son-in-law, Lucy's husband, was a member."

"Pardon me, madam," said Poe, "but what was his name?"

"Joseph Brody. But he's dead. You see, my son-in-law was in on a criminal arrangement of some sort with the Butchers and tried to cheat them. Soon after, Lucy was found dead, killed the same way as Mary, with a cleaver."

"I see," said Poe. "A reprisal. What about your son-in-law?"

"He vanished, and later I heard that he had been killed as well."

"Where did you hear that?"

"Why, Mary told me. I'd wait for her until early in the morning when she returned from vending, and then we'd take tea together and she'd tell me all about what had happened that evening and night—the gossip on the streets, and the important news. Then we'd turn to the Bible. She had heard that Joe had been killed. The news of his death did not make either of us unhappy, God forgive us. He was a brutal, stupid man who often beat my Lucy, and a criminal, and even a cheat among his criminal friends, which brought about Lucy's death, and now the death of my sweet Mary."

"The same weapon in both cases," I said.

"Yes," said Poe, "but how long ago was your daughter Lucy murdered, madam?"

"It's been five years. Lucy was twenty-one."

"How old was Mary?"

"Twenty-one."

"Then Mary was sixteen when Lucy was murdered?"

"Yes."

"Why should the gang strike at Mary?" asked Poe. "And why should they have waited so long? And why should they do so after Joe Brody's death? What benefit would there be to them in killing Mary?"

"There's something wrong there," I said.

"But who else would want to kill Mary?" asked Mrs. Hart. "And who else but the Butchers would use such a weapon?"

"That, my dear lady," said Poe, "is the question."

"But it couldn't have been Mr. VanBrunt," said Mrs. Hart. "Mary told me that she intended to marry him. My Mary was an honest girl and a good judge of decency in people. She told me many times what a fine man Mr. VanBrunt was, that he came from a respected family, and that he would deal honestly with her. We had hopes that he would find a life for me, as well. It was our dream that Mary should find a man like him. Certainly he would have no reason, no reason at all, to want to do such a thing to her. He could simply say that he was done with courting her, and Mary's pride would put an end to things."

"We agree with you," said Poe, "that Mr. VanBrunt is innocent, and I can say that he held your Mary in the highest esteem. If it's any consolation to you, it's a fact that he intended to propose marriage to Mary on the day of her death."

"Ma'am," I said, "what happened immediately after the death of your daughter, Lucy? I mean, before you heard of Joe Brody's death?"

"What happened? Let me see. Well, Joe quit the gang, that's what he told Mary. Mary told me that Joe quit in order to redeem himself, although it seemed out of character to me."

"Can you describe your son-in-law—physically?" asked Poe.

"My sight's been gone for many years, young man. I never saw him. He was described to me, of course. Tall, nice looking. But I didn't like his voice. There was cruelty, stupidity in it. I'm sorry I can't be of too much help."

"It's too soon to say that you haven't been," said Poe.

"On the contrary," said I. "I think you've been of great help, Mrs. Hart. This gang business puts a new cast to things."

"Did Mary dislike Joe Brody as much as you did?" asked Poe, getting to his feet.

"She loathed him. I think he was attracted to Mary, though she was just a child then. I suspected as much from certain conversations I overheard between Lucy and Mary."

"Was Lucy jealous of Mary?" I asked.

"No, no. Not over Joe."

"How, then? In some other way?"

"There was a bit of rivalry between the girls over me, I think. Before Joe came into the picture the girls and I had been very close. Lucy, being the eldest, I depended upon. But when she left to marry Joe, Mary took her place as my strong right arm. As I said, Mary would read to me from the Bible every morning. One day Lucy came over and gave me *this* Bible, that I hold in my hand. It was inscribed to me, she said, and it was never to be read by Mary, or anyone else, except herself, when *she* was reading it to me. Jealousy? Not exactly. As I say, it was a sort of rivalry over me that this Bible business showed. That's an example. But I kept my word to Lucy. I never let Mary read from Lucy's Bible. And I never let it out of my hands, as I promised her I wouldn't.

"No, no. Lucy did not blame Mary for the behavior of her husband. She warned Mary not to be alone with Joe. Mary, as I said, was only just growing into womanhood. Lucy and Joe had been married for several years, and Joe had been around to see Mary grow up. Both Lucy and I were afraid of

66

Joe, and afraid for Mary with regard to him. He was capable of anything."

I looked at Poe, who nodded.

"We thank you very much, Mrs. Hart, for the tea, and for your help," I said, rising.

"After Lucy's death," said Mrs. Hart, "or, actually, after Mary told me that Joe had been killed, I made her swear on this Bible that she would never mention him to me again, never use his name in my presence, and this is the first time in nearly five years that I've used his name. The very mention of it used to make me sick. That should make clear to you gentlemen how determined I am to be of help."

"Again," said Poe, "we thank you, madam."

## Chapter 14

## BAITS AND TRAPS

Outside, the November day was growing unseasonably warm and sunny. Had I been in Greenwich Village, or, even more so, in my country haunts, I should have appreciated the warmth; but when heat struck the slums surrounding the Five Points, the manure in the streets and the night-soil in the alleys ripened with energy. In summer the stench could prove unbearable. Here and now it remained at an acceptable level. Flies would be abounding if the heat continued. What we needed was snow, but, alas, that would bring more smoke. Poe sniffed the air with nervous nostrils.

"What have you got in mind?" he asked.

I apprised Poe of a few facts regarding Boodle Coign. "He's a member of the Plug Uglies," I said, "and a pigeon, an informer. Perhaps he can shed some light on the relationship of the gang to the murder of Lucy Hart Brody, to the possible murder of Joe Brody—we can't be entirely certain of that—and to the murder of Mary Hart. There *must* be a connecting link!"

"Let's hope he can," said Poe, his face grey in the drench of sunlight. "To know the exact nature of that link would be, perhaps, to resolve the matter."

"It's bull-baiting day at Bunker Hill, and Boodle Coign is an owner, and dedicated to the filthy entertainment. Have you ever seen it?"

"Not *seen*—but heard of it, of course. How's it done?"

"A bull is chained to a swivel ring and dogs torment him. The sport is to wager on the number of dogs the bull will gore. Boodle will be there, it's certain, and I think it would be wise to go there and have a few words with him."

"Did I hear you say Bunker Hill?"

"Yes, sir. *Our* Bunker Hill is up near Greenwich Village. A fort was built there during the Revolution, and defended against General Howe. Later, a Fly Market butcher named Winship built an arena inside the fort for bull-baiting."

"Oh, yes, I have heard of it," said Poe. "I've spent a good deal of time, off and on, in the city, but I've never been to the old fort."

"It was my thought, sir, that you might take Danny Devlin with you back to Red Kate's and keep an eye on him while I went on to Bunker Hill and spoke to Boodle Coign."

"If I am to be of any assistance in this matter, I must hear for myself what is said."

"In that case, sir, I think we must deposit little Devlin in good hands somewhere, because it would be wrong to take him into the midst of such a crowd."

"Nor," said Poe, "dare we leave him at Red Kate's. Red Kate herself may be our killer, and that would be like presenting the lamb to the wolf."

"You suspect her to such a degree?"

"It's a matter of motive," said Poe. "If VanBrunt did not kill Mary Hart in a drunken rage, because she rejected him—and we know from Mrs. Hart that Mary intended to accept his proposal, if proffered—*then*, who else had reason to kill her? The Butcher's Gang? Would they persist in revenge five years later?"

"It's possible."

"Anything is possible. But we must deal in *probabilities*, not mere *possibilities*, which place us all-at-sea. Until we know more we must work with what we have. I cannot believe that Mary Hart's death was random—a robbery or some such—not when the weapon used was a replica of one used to murder her sister five years earlier. That, though *possibly* coincidental, is not *probably* coincidental. It appears to be symbolic. After all—a butcher's cleaver—in both cases! Therefore I look for motive and come up with Red Kate's jealousy. It is to be hoped that jealousy is not our last word on the subject—but it *is* all we have for a motive. After all, who had such a girl offended?"

"I agree that Red Kate might be capable of murdering a rival, in business or in love, but do you believe her capable of murdering a crippled boy, however unpleasant, like the Gimp?"

Poe sighed. "It's too much to doubt that the murder of the Gimp is not connected with Mary Hart's murder, for there in the middle of both murders our friend VanBrunt is to be found. Clearly, he's a central part of the condition. Clearly, too, he did not knock himself out."

"But consider, Mr. Poe. VanBrunt was drunk when he went to Paradise Square to propose. Suppose Mary did reject him because he was drinking?"

"Are you acting the Devil's advocate?" asked Poe, smiling.

"Shouldn't one of us?"

"But, Sergeant, how can a man kill a woman and *then* run toward her scream?"

# Chapter 15

## THE STREET URCHIN

Walking through the Bloody Ould Sixth Ward at ten o'clock of a midweek morning was like walking through rip-roaring hell. Dance-houses, diving bells, and other dens of iniquity were booming. Near them the smell of alcohol overwhelmed the stench of miasma. Banjos banged, drums beat, horns blasted. Swarms of rag-footed, little tatterdemalions were underfoot. Pigs rolled in mud, oinking, or followed at your heels, begging a handout, like the innumerable thin mangy dogs of the area. Rats foraged, insouciantly. A dead horse was beaten by a cabman while several butchers gathered at the scene, cleavers in hand, and, behind them, hungry enough to be bold, a mob of the poor of both sexes, several races, and all ages collected like vultures for what remained when the butchers were satisfied.

In the center of the Five Points the women had arrived at Paradise Square with their wet rags. It was a good day for laundry. Clouds, like bunches of silken balloons, scudded across the blue, bird-peppered sky. Some of the laundry still steamed on the palings. The plutocrats among the poor handed out cornbread to the stave- or brickbat-bearing boys who would stand guard for them. Thus the lucky were assured of one small meal that day.

"There's Devlin," I said.

The ragged, dirty little boy stood before the laundry-festooned fence, smoking a cigar.

"It's youse again," he greeted us. "Youse'll get nothin' out o' me."

He was about four and a half feet tall and so light that he lifted off his feet when I collared him.

"You are going to visit some very nice people who would not approve of your cigar." I flung the rolled tobacco into the street, where a mob of mop-headed urchins materialized to fight over it.

"Now see what ya done!"

"Come along," I said, "you little wolf's whelp! Do you have anyone to stay with? Where you'll be safe?"

"I'm a orphan."

"We'll take him to the mission," I said. "They'll keep an eye on him there."

"Oh, naw!" cried Devlin. "I hate them psalm-singers."

I knelt down before the boy and shook him by the shoulders. "Listen, my little man, there is somebody who may try to do you in. Do you understand?"

"What? Me?"

"You know something important about the murder of the Hot Corn Girl."

73

"I don't know nothin'.'"

"You know that the man who is accused of it probably didn't do it."

"How do *you* know?"

"We have our methods." I winked at Poe, who was looking sadly down at the boy.

"You know," I went on, "that the girl screamed, and was probably attacked, before the accused man had entered the park. You know that, don't you? Admit it!"

"So what?"

"So *what*, is that the murderer may know you know it, and may therefore want to do you in. Understand?"

"Jeese!" He stopped struggling and seemed inclined to co-operate.

"You know I'm the law. See, here's my star."

"What you want I should do?"

"Just behave yourself and come along. And don't say *Jeese*. They won't like it at the mission."

One group or other of social reformers always had an out-post in the Five Points. The latest was the A.I.C.P., or, the Association for Improving the Condition of the Poor. Many of the members were influential women whose male friends

74

and relatives were wealthy. They were determined to see change in the Five Points. One specific and oft-stated goal was to tear down the Old Brewery, which they considered the source of the depravity that infected the area, and to build on its site a grand new mission house. At this time, however, they were located in a small, clapboard building on Little Water Street, off the Five Points.

# Chapter 16

## I FIND MY LOVE

Inside, several pretty Hot Corn Girls were engaged in finance with a man of about forty years of age who sat at a table counting stacks of coins. I stepped doubtfully up to the table, Devlin in tow, and asked of the man, "Is this the Association for Improving the Condition of the Poor?"

"He looked up from his business with a benign smile. "It is, sir, or rather it is one small outpost of our organization. Thadeus Thorndyke, at your service. What can I do for you?"

I told him my purpose, adding the question: "Are you a concessionaire?"

"I am a lay minister, sir—*and*, in the name of charity, a concessionaire." He addressed himself momentarily to the young ladies. "That's fine now. Until later, my dears. Report at the usual time this afternoon. Have faith in our Lord, who can make you money and keep you honest at once." The young women retreated.

"Now, sir. I see you are taken aback. Let me explain. We operate a hot corn concession for a two-fold purpose, first, to give the girls honest work and earnings, thus keeping them free from temptation and fostering their inherent honesty, and, second, to add to the coffers of the mission, to enhance its work."

"I see. I'd like to question the girls about Mary Hart."

"Oh, terrible thing, that! A lovely and innocent child, devil take her murderer, though God forgive him!" He looked down and back up. "The girls will be back at five o'clock to pick up their wares. It's getting near the end of our season."

"Are you one of the directors of this mission?"

"No, sir. I am but a helper. But you're in luck. Dr. Whitney, the Director of this outpost, is in back. I'll get her."

I looked at Poe, who pursed his lips. "Interesting," he said.

I could not know it, but one of the great moments of my life was about to flicker and pass into memory, the moment I laid entranced eyes upon the woman who would become my wife. She stepped out before Mr. Thorndyke from the back room, a woman in her early thirties, tall, well-formed, face tanned and radiant with physical health, eyes clear and blue and confident, hair upswept and piled in an amorphous light-brown crown.

"What can I do for you, sir?" she asked.

I was struck dumb. Poe intervened.

"Madam," he said, stepping in, "we've come to you for assistance with regard to the temporary safe-keeping of this boy." He took Devlin's cap from his head. "But allow me to present myself and my friends. I am Edgar Poe, this is Sergeant Jonathan Goode of the Municipal Police, and our young friend here is Master Daniel Devlin."

"Edgar Poe," said Dr. Whitney. "Would you happen to be Mr. Edgar *Allan* Poe, the author and poet, the editor of *Graham's Magazine*?"

"Yes, madam, I am that Mr. Poe, but that *former* editor."

"But, Mr. Poe, I am Eleanor Whitney."

Poe looked puzzled.

"Eleanor *Vance* Whitney. You once accepted several of my poems for *Graham's*."

"Of *course*," said Poe, his eyes lighting with recognition. "You're the author of that very powerful poem about the Old Brewery, 'Heathen House'."

"It is my intention to use all means at my command to rid the world of that horror," said my lovely, vehemently. A determined and talented woman.

"As I said, madam—a *powerful* poem. It enlisted my interest in your cause—and, indeed," Poe went on, "to such an extent that I have lately made a tour of your 'Heathen House' to see the conditions you described at first hand, as did my friend, Mr. Dickens—and about which he wrote in his 'American Notes.'" He glanced at me, furtively. "I also consider your poem about the late and much-to-be-lamented *Mr.* Whitney to be of great worth. It touched me more deeply, as I have recently myself suffered a grievous loss."

"I am sorry to hear that, Mr. Poe."

"My young wife, madam. An angel who trod on earth."

"We grieve together, then," said Eleanor Whitney. "But it has been, alas, some time since my husband passed on."

"The immediacy of your poem gave me to think that you were only recently bereaved."

"These things do not pass so readily, Mr. Poe. But I need not tell you. Forgive me."

"Not at all, madam. And how charming it is in these circumstances to meet with a fellow poet."

"But I am humbled before you, Mr. Poe. You are one of the great lyric voices of our age. However, I must admit to you something. Please don't be offended. It's just that I find your tales and stories to be—to be—"

"Morbid?"

She sighed. "Just so."

"You're not alone, madam. I write out of the German tradition of the Tales of A.T.E. Hoffmann, and I do so perhaps provoked by a world that contains an Old Brewery—or bull-baiting."

"I do not quite follow—"

"Excuse me," I said. "But we must explain our purpose. We are on an errand."

"Please, do explain!"

"We understand from Mrs. Hart, Mary's mother—Mary Hart who was killed in Paradise Square, and who worked for your association—"

"Yes, yes, I understand."

"—that you have been looking in on her, tending her in her need."

"Yes. We're trying to find a home for her."

"This boy was a witness to the murder, and we have reason to believe that he might be in danger. I was wondering if you could keep an eye on him while Mr. Poe and I go to investigate a matter pertaining to the case?"

"Certainly, Sergeant. I shall be happy to do so."

For the first time she looked at me full in the face, and my heart fell in my chest to see that there was no unusual sign of interest in her candid eyes.

## Chapter 17

## BULL-BAITING

The swivel-tied bull was scrawny, hollow of flank and knobby of joint. The dogs were at him snarling, tearing. A great devil of a dog tore a strip of muscle from the bull's flank. Blood gushed there, a red stripe. But immediately the enraged bull caught the dog with its horns and tossed it broken and squealing into the air. Poe slowly turned a stony-faced, contemptuous head, looking at the faces in the crowd. "What manner of beasts are these?" he said at last.

"Follow me to the owners," I said, "and see for yourself. But have a great care. We are on dangerous ground."

We made our way through the crowd to the owners' stalls, where more bellowing bulls, more barking dogs, and more cackling human types, awaited their turns. I spotted Boodle Coign among a group of owners.

"I must call him out," I told Poe, "and it will be risky. It must seem that I'm accusing him of something so that the others won't suspect him of informing. But if I press him too hard, the others might come down on us like wolves, to protect him. A delicate balance. Stand clear until I get him alone."

I pinned my star to my coat and plunged into the group. "Coign, I want to have a word with you about some missing jewels."

The group closed on me. I'm a burly man, but these Plug Uglies were famous for their size and ferocity. I took Boodle by the arm, as if to lead him away, and found myself completely encircled by Plug-hatted thugs. Boodle came to my rescue, as I'd hoped he would.

"It's okay, lads," he said. "This Friday-faced booly dog's got nothin' on me. I'll talk to him."

A space was made just large enough for us to walk through. I led Boodle over to Poe.

"Make it quick," said the Butcher under his breath.

"I'm collecting a debt, Boodle."

He shrugged. "Let's have it."

I told him, quickly.

"About Mary Hart's murder," he said, "I only know what I read in the papers. I do know something about Lucy Hart's murder, though. She was married to a Plug Ugly."

I nodded.

"Anyhow," he said, looking nervously about, "the cove's name was Joe Brody—"

"We've got that."

"Well, Joe Brody got the bright idea to threaten Boss Meade by going to this journalist, Russell McNeil, and giving him some inside information, see?"

"Go on."

"But Boss Meade don't scare. Instead he tells the Butchers what Brody is trying to pull. They hack Brody's evil," he looked Poe over—"his wife, see—and they cut his conk."

"His conk?" said Poe.

Boodle tapped his nose with a long-nailed index.

"No-Nose," I said.

"But why didn't they kill Joe Brody?" asked Poe.

"No pain in that," said Boodle. "They hack up his wife and leave him to walk around without a nose, remembering. From what I hear, this Joe Brody was a ben—"

"A what?" asked Poe.

"A fool. Crafty, see, but a stupid cove. He had to be, to try a trick like that on Boss Meade."

"Do you know anything at all about Mary Hart?" I asked him.

"No; I told you."

"She was Joe Brody's sister-in-law," said Poe.

"She was? I don't know nothin' about it. Now you better let me go. They're watching us." I turned him loose. "Crushers don't get nothin' from me but a fibbing fist," he called out so his cohorts could hear, and marched off.

"What do you think?" I asked Poe.

"We have to have a long talk with No-Nose Mullins. But before we do, I'd like to have another look at the arena. I may want to pen some story with such a setting."

I had in my possession a Cuban cigar, which I drew from my vest and lit. I had been touched by Poe calling me friend. There was much in him that was different, unlike others, unique; it was the poet in him; and there was much in him too that was clear and understandable and admirable to a plain man like myself; viz., his courage, his honesty, his sense of honor, his courtesy, his kindness, particularly in evidence toward those whose minds were in relation to his as those of an order so much lower as to be different in kind. What went on in that complex mind? Perhaps it was not the thing in itself that he was looking at, the bull-baiting, but some ghostly meaning behind, beyond it. Much of the time there was something other-worldly about him, and sometimes I felt the need to draw him back, almost as if in fear that he should be permanently lost. I smoked my cigar for a quarter of an hour while Poe's eyes went from the ring to the crowd and back in a constant oscillation. Finally, he said: "How many are here, do you suppose?"

"Fourteen, fifteen hundred of the most vicious and dangerous coves and molls in the Frog and Toe, as they would call the City of New York. Come, Mr. Poe. We must be on to see Mr. McNeil of *The Broadway Star*."

# Chapter 18

## PLUG-UGLIES

We stepped out of the fortification and had gone a few steps across the muddy sod, when we were accosted by two plug-hatted giants, who were clearly up to no good.

"Back off!" I said, and took my pistol from my pocket. But one of the brutes outpaced me, slapping the pistol from my hand with the flat of a cleaver, which he immediately drew back and struck me with flatly across the hairline.

I awoke in a dimly-lit chamber which I could identify as a room in the fortification by the mossy stones of its narrow walls. The dim light came from whale-oil lamps, and the reek of the burning whale-oil was sickening in such close quarters. I shut my eyes and opened them again, and saw opposite me a bloodied figure chained to a wall. For a moment I thought I was having visions of our Savior, for my mind was dazed and my head pounded in tempo to an urgent tom-tom. I heard rough voices. Then I understood my situation. I was sprawled in a chair. The chair was in the middle of the room. The man on the wall was Boodle Coign, one of his ears cut off, blood streaming to the floor. Poe was nowhere to be seen.

Great fingers snaked into my hair and yanked my head back.

"He's awake." It was the man who had hit me.

He smeared his hand down my face, and I could smell blood, *my* blood. Consciousness deserted me, but returned immediately.

I pulled my feet under me and struggled forward, only to be pushed back. I shook my head and rubbed my eyes and looked at my hands, which were wet and sticky and red.

"What's that for?" I asked, indicating the man on the wall with a painful nod.

"He's a pigeon, as if I had to tell *you*. We suspicioned him for quite some time."

The other brute loomed before me. "You'll get the same, if you don't sing sweet, copper."

"Didn't you get it from *him*?"

"He told us you was interested in Joe Brody, his wife, and about that Hot Corn Girl what was kilt."

"Well?"

"Well, this: What's it all about? What you want to know about something that happened five years ago? What about the Hot Corn Girl?"

"You better talk, copper, or off with your ears." He menaced me with a cleaver, slashing down the left side of my head and then down the right within centimeters of my ears.

"It's the cleaver," I said, hoping to give them something to think about while *I* was thinking about how I could make my escape.

"The cleaver?"

"You boys carry cleavers. The Hot Corn Girl was murdered with a cleaver."

"Half of the blokes out in the arena is butchers. Dey all got cleavers. What's dat come to?"

"Boodle told us—" I thought of Poe. "Where's my friend?"

"Sleeping out on da sod."

"Did you . . . Was he hurt?"

"I snitchelled his gig," said the second brute, meaning he smashed his nose.

"We went over him," said the first brute, still waving the cleaver. "He ain't no copper—no star. Who is he?"

"A writer. A friend."

"A scribbler? I told you he wasn't worth draggin' in."

The first brute said:

"I ast you, what's it come to dat a mort was butchered?"

"She was Joe Brody's wife's sister," I told him.

They looked puzzled.

After a pause, the first brute said:

"Boodle went out before he told us dat."

He looked at the other, wrinkling his low brow into a washboard. He turned on me:

"You are saying—do I understand right? You are saying dat who kilt da mort, dis was de same as who kilt Joe Brody's wife?"

"Could be," I said. "We know the Butchers are an inside group in the Plug Uglies. They deal with politics—double voting, stuffing ballot boxes, or losing them. They're Boss Meade's personal strong arm boys. They carry cleavers hung by leather thongs from their belts—like you boys. We know that the Butcher's Gang killed Lucy Hart Brody and committed mayhem on Joe Brody."

I could think of nothing to talk about but the case. I had run it through my mind so many times I could recite my thoughts about it and think about a mode of escape at the same time. I reasoned that I wasn't telling them anything they didn't know, if they were guilty; and that, if they were not involved in Mary Hart's death, I might stir them to say something useful. Meantime, I considered the possibilities. Should I brace myself and make a headlong charge for the door? Should I feign unconsciousness and catch them off-guard? "And we find it difficult to believe," I rambled on, "that Lucy and Mary Hart could be murdered by the same weapon, even if five years apart, and there not be a connection." I cried out, as if in pain, and slumped in my chair, closing my eyes.

"Rats!" came the voice of the first brute, "I must have hit him harder dan I taught. Get some water, Legs."

"Rather, gentlemen, disarm yourselves—and *quickly!*"

Poe stood in the doorway, pistol in hand. Blood oozed from his nose.

"Are you all right?" I wheezed, kicking an assortment of weapons toward the door.

"I shall have no need of an ivory conk," he said. "Would you be good enough to check on Coign, Sergeant?"

I felt Coign's chest. "He's alive," I said. Coign's arms were merely looped over the chains and I had no difficulty extricating him, so that his great beaten bulk fell heavily across my shoulders.

"Wait, Sergeant. We came here for information. You Butchers wanted to find out what Boodle told us. He told us that the Butcher's Gang killed Joe Brody's wife, Lucy. How about a fair exchange?"

"Why not?" said the brute called Legs. "You ain't gettin' out of here."

"We shall see," said Poe. "What do you know about Lucy Brody's death?"

"Sure. It was me and Butt, here, went up there that morning to get Joe Brody. We found him sitting over his wife's body. He done it."

"Why did Joe Brody kill his wife?"

"A bunch of the boys got drunk that Friday night," said Legs. "I was there, and so was Butt. They started teasing him about his wife and Meade. He left angry, and dead drunk. We never figured he'd kill her. But when we went there Sunday morning, she was dead. He must have done it that Friday night, judging from the state of her body."

"Fair enough," said Poe. "Let's go, Sergeant."

"We won't let you leave here with Coign, you know," said Butt.

I stepped out into the dark passageway, stubbing my toes on cleavers, pistols, brass knuckles, and black jacks. Poe backed out after me, pulling the heavy door shut.

"The fittings are here for a padlock," he said, groping at the door, "but I can't find one. Sergeant, have you got hand-cuffs?"

I balanced Coign's weight on my shoulders and reached an arm behind me, found my cuffs, and handed them to Poe, who looped a cuff into the padlock fitting.

"That should hold them," he said. "Lead on, Sergeant!"

I chose a direction, not knowing in the dim light any better way out than Poe would have known.

# Chapter 19

## LIGHT AT THE END OF THE TUNNEL

Before we had gone twenty paces the Butchers set up a noisy protest at our backs. They called for help, banged at the door, and heaved something heavy at it. The sounds of their angry, determined efforts reverberated down the stony passageways after us, echoing even ahead of us, so that, like bats in the dark, we could feel the walls before us.

"If someone hears," I said, panting, "they'll have an army upon us."

"Where is the way out, Sergeant?" cried Poe.

"Sir, I do not know! I only know that the other way goes into it."

But ahead there was light—faint light.

"What's that?"

"Take a turn, sir," I cried.

We came upon a glorious sight—a window, outside of which the day was bright with sun. But closer, and we saw that it was grated inside and barred outside.

"There is no way out here," said Poe.

Now we could hear the clattering of feet behind us, at some distance. "The place is a maze in the dark," said Poe.

"Let's hope that they've taken a wrong turn," I said.

"If so," said Poe, "the only way to undo our error is to continue in it beyond its power to confound us."

"Sir?"

"William Blake said that if a fool persists in his folly he will become wise."

"Sir?" I was exasperated, and about to say so. "Good heavens, Poe!—"

"We must go *through* the window," said Poe, who had begun to pry at the grating with the pistol. "This is an old fortification, and the weather of years has weakened its fixtures." The grate snapped, and Poe lifted it out. "Rust," he mumbled, "the Conqueror Worm of iron."

Voices sounded like an off-key choir.

"They're getting closer, sir!"

"I hear," said Poe, working at the window. He shattered pane after pane of glass with the pistol, then knocked out the woodwork. "Everything is old here," he said, "and rotted, and the country is but barely sixty."

"Sir?"

"A thought, Sergeant. I can see the masonry. It's quite weak. It was made for pressure from the outside, not inside. Ugh. I haven't the strength, Sergeant. Put Coign down and lend a shoulder here."

I joined Poe in pushing against the bars. We had, in a moment, established a rhythm, heave-ho, as it were, and felt a give, another, and a release of the bars, all in a grill, with a clang and a soft thump as they fell to the ground outside. We turned back to see a wavering light.

"I'll climb through," said Poe. "You hand Coign out."

I retrieved Coign's inert body and plunged it, helter-skelter through the window. I could hear Poe's efforts below.

Suddenly the hall brightened at my back, torch light merging with that from the window.

"There!" came a cry as I leaped. A ball whizzed above my dropping head.

I gathered up Coign.

"This way," cried Poe. "There's a carriage."

Poe ran ahead and opened the carriage door. I heaved Coign's bulk inside and climbed in after. Poe jumped into the open door, but hung outward, and cried to the driver, "Off with you! Go!

Go!"

A shot was fired from the window.

"Not me," said the driver. "Get away from my carriage!" A horse whip snapped down across Poe's back. He raised the pistol.

"Go, sir, or damn me, I'll blow your head off."

The carriage lurched, began to roll, gained speed, and plummeted ahead, Poe still hanging on. It was only when the carriage approached a more civilized section of the city, and Poe was certain that we had lost any pursuers, that he called for a halt. "I can shoot you off your seat through the carriage roof as well as from out here, sir," he said to the driver, and joined me inside. "What now?"

"They've beaten Coign almost to death," I said.

Poe leaned out the window and cried:

"To the hospital!"

Now the carriage moved forward at a clip.

"How did you find me?" I said.

Poe wiped blood from his nose with his handkerchief. He was ashen, bloodless but for the red ooze at his upper lip, and soaking wet, though a mild November breeze rushed in the carriage windows. Outside, some of the pleasanter parts of the city could be seen.

"I knew they couldn't have taken you far. Why should they? They were among fifteen hundred of their own. If they took you, they must have done so to question you. That, they

94

would not do in a crowd—therefore, one of the cells in the fortification."

"Where did you get the pistol?"

"It's yours. When I was struck I threw myself upon it. The devil of it was keeping it under me when I was searched."

"But why didn't you use the pistol when they were taking me away?"

"I hoped that there was something to be learned. I didn't intend to allow enough time to go by for you to be further injured. But you were quite unconscious. They should have to revive you first."

"You are a handy man to have around, Mr. Poe."

"But, bethink yourself, sir—had I used the weapon earlier, I should have been faced with a serious situation. Two toughs with raised hands, and an unconscious policeman, too heavy for me to lift, surrounded by enemies. No, sir, it was better that I did as I did."

"You mistake me, Poe," I said. "There was no irony in what I said. You are, indeed, a handy man!"

Mr. Poe did not take a compliment well, I saw, for now his face held a tinge of color.

# Chapter 20

## PHYSICIAN, HEAL THYSELF

At the City Hospital we turned Boodle Coign over to the attention of physicians, and were ourselves treated for various abrasions. The blood was staunched in its flow from Poe's nose by the infusion of some unpleasant stuff, or so he told me. My head and hand were bandaged.

We went to have a look at VanBrunt, who remained unconscious.

"Is it all right?" I asked the doctor. "He has been thus for several hours now."

"With a concussion it's difficult to say. He could stay this way for a day—or forever."

"Physician, heal thyself!" said Poe bitterly.

"Sir?" The doctor looked at him.

"You speak in pathetic clichés," said Poe. "In your field, as in most, men of genius are few, and such are the only ones who can do humanity any good. My young wife is dead at the hands of physicians, whose ministrations, though no medico myself, I have been able, by virtue only of a mind that reasons, to see for the barbarisms that they were. Indeed, living on this earth is like living with stupid demons."

"Sir!" The doctor stood amazed at Poe's outburst, as I myself was.

He turned on his heel and strode out through the door.

"I apologize for my friend," I said to the doctor. "He has undergone great difficulties and is not quite himself. Is there a place where he and I might wash ourselves and comb our hair?"

"Down the hall," said the doctor woodenly.

We had told our carriage driver to wait, but we found him gone.

"Poe," I said, "why don't you go back to Red Kate's and get some rest. You were awakened by being shot at early this morning and you'd had little rest before that. Since then, we've been through all manner of difficulties and stresses, and, sir, you don't look at all well. Let's walk until we find a hack. I'll put you aboard, you go to our rooms, have something to eat, and get some sleep. What do you say?"

"I say, sir, that *The Broadway Star* is just around the corner."

## Chapter 21

## THE NEWS HOUND

The *Broadway Star* was in Newspaper Row between James Gordon Bennett's *Herald* and Horace Greeley's *Tribune*, a mouse between two elephants. We were told McNeil's office was on the second floor. There we found a short, burly, intense man with walrus mustaches, smoking a thick green cigar. He stared at us through owlish, silver-rimmed spectacles. I showed him my star and introduced myself and Poe.

"Poe?" he said. Interest formed where none had been. "Edgar Allan Poe?"

"I am he," said Poe.

"The poet, Poe?"

"The same."

"Well, sir," said McNeil, "a fellow writer. How interesting!"

"First, sir, a poet, then a writer, then a journalist," said Poe, slowly. "But, yes—a writer. I am an old hand in Printing House Square. I worked in the publication office of the *New York Mirror*, on Ann and Nassau Streets."

"I see," said McNeil, with a puzzled look on his face.

"There *are* distinctions," said Poe.

I suspected, as I believed McNeil was beginning to suspect, that Poe had insulted him. Poe was not helping our cause by offending McNeil. I broke in:

"We would like to have a word with you."

"I was just going out to eat," said McNeil coolly, as he gathered his things to leave.

"May we join you?" I asked.

He pursed his lips, grimaced, eyed Poe, and relaxed suddenly.

"Come ahead then," he said. "I am an admirer of Mr. Poe. I'd like to discuss his writing over an ale."

He took us to Fraunces Tavern at Broad and Pearl Streets. The place was crowded, festive almost, with its steamy, pungent smell of good food and drink. We took a corner table and ate with intermittent small talk. McNeil and I had good roast beef. Poe would have none of it, he said, after witnessing a bull-baiting. He ate minimally from a seafood platter, and drank amply of heavy dark ale.

"Bull-baiting," said McNeil, pushing back an empty plate. "It's a brute's sport, if sport it is to set a pack of hounds to torment a dying bull. It's something I'm going to write a series of articles about. I'll break the thing up, if I can."

"You are a genuine reformer, then, sir?" I said.

"I mean business," shot McNeil. "What did you imagine?"

"Well, sir," said Poe, "we journalists know the merit of a lurid tale."

"Circulation? Well, my stories make money, yes, if that's a crime; but I mean business, sir. I mean to have them out!"

"Who?" I asked.

"The corruptors. The politicians who use the gangs like swords hanging fire. I mean business, sir. I mean to have them out!"

"Highly commendable," said Poe.

"Well—" puffed McNeil. I thanked God that Poe had decided on tact.

I told McNeil what Boodle Coign knew about Joe Brody.

"Yes, Brody came to see me, but it wasn't much. He informed me that there was a connection between the gangs and the politicians, one in particular—Boss Meade."

"And—"

"And nothing. I told him that any fool knew that the Plug Uglies were connected to Meade. Meade's a respectable character now, if a political boss in the Five Points can be called such, but he came out of their ranks—first a butcher, many years ago, later a gang member, and now a politician, well known at City Hall. I told Brody that what I needed of

100

a man such as himself—to be frank, a cutthroat—I needed evidence, proof positive."

"What did he say?"

"He seemed rather surprised at my reaction. I think he actually thought that it was news that Boss Meade and the Plug Uglies were tied up. He struck me as a stupid fellow. An improviser, but not a very astute one. So then, as if he were throwing me a carrot, he told me that Meade had lived for some time with a mort who had claim of being his common law wife. When Meade began to rise in politics, he bought her off by giving her the wherewithal to go into business as a saloon keeper. He didn't give me her name. It was implied that that was one gift he might offer me. It would have been useful, but not very."

I felt Poe's boot nudge under the table, hesitated, then said something other than I had intended to say.

"Joe Brody's wife was murdered," I said.

"Yes," said McNeil, "Lucy. Axed, wasn't she?"

"Cleavered," I said.

"Because of his visit to me, do you suppose?"

"Directly."

"Really!" McNeil pursed his lips, blew. "But he hadn't told me anything. Look, I'll be forthcoming with you, but I want the same. As a matter of fact, Brody said that he had his wife's diary, incriminating to Meade."

"What did he ask for?"

"Wanted the paper to give him some money for the story."

"How much?"

"He was—indefinite. It was rather vague, really, what he wanted."

"He wanted nothing," said Poe.

"Nothing? I don't quite—"

"He wanted nothing," Poe repeated.

I said: "He wasn't selling a story. Don't you see? He was going to put the screws to Boss Meade. Blackmail. You were his threat."

"I say—he *was* an addle-cove, wasn't he? I mean, to take on a bad bloke like Meade!"

"Meade came down on him like a hammer. He had Joe Brody's wife brutally murdered, and Brody's nose—amputated—"

"I thought Brody was dead," said McNeil.

"He is," said Poe, "in a sense. He now wears an ivory—*conk*, and is known as No-Nose Mullins."

"He's one I don't know," said McNeil. "I mean, I *knew* Brody, but never heard of this No-Nose character."

"I read your piece on the murder of Mary Hart," said Poe. "Mary Hart is—was—Lucy Brody's sister."

"The cleaver again," said McNeil.

"The cleaver again," said Poe.

"When I wrote that piece, I had spoken only to the leather-head who arrested VanBrunt. It seemed an open and shut case. A crime of passion. VanBrunt, mad with drink, could not accept rejection, and killed the girl. I was bothered by the weapon, but there was even a witness, a crippled kid, wasn't there?"

"He's dead—strangled," I said.

"Do you see a connection there? After all, life is very, very cheap in the Five Points."

"There is a connection," said Poe. "How could there not be, when Mary Hart's presumed murderer, Peter VanBrunt, was found comatose at the scene of the crippled boy's murder?"

"My God!" cried McNeil. "What's going on here?"

"That's the question," said Poe.

McNeil sat in thought for a moment, then said:

"You know, I wrote to the VanBrunt family—a gesture, you see—"

"To what effect?" asked Poe.

"I told them that he was in trouble. I sent them a copy of the newspaper piece on the murder. I thought the poor devil should have at least benefit of counsel. I understand that he's penniless."

"Did they respond?" I asked.

"They sent back that they would have nothing whatsoever to do with him."

"Loyalty," said Poe—"rhymes with royalty. The VanBrunts may be aristocrats but they are something less than royalty at its best, from which one expects noblesse oblige, at least."

"Speak not to me of royalty," said McNeil heatedly. "I'm an Irishman."

"So am I," said Poe. "But a Southerner."

"So am I," said McNeil. "But a Yankee."

Each glared at the other. Then laughed.

# Chapter 22

## AN INVITATION

We found Dr. Whitney, the sleeves of her dress rolled up, filling oaken buckets with hot, roasted corn. "Ah, Sergeant Goode, Mr. Poe." She stopped work and drew us aside.

"That poor little Devlin! He told me about himself. What a sad tale! He remembers a cottage in Ireland—a voyage aboard a crowded ship—then very little—then being in care of one or another foster parent—and finally living on his own, hand to mouth. He thinks his parents are dead. He's been living in a box. Actually living in a wooden crate! He's an intelligent little fellow. What can we do to help him? There *is* an orphanage . . . . Oh, it disturbs me!"

She threw up her hands, then said: "Despite our best efforts, between twenty and sixty thousand children in this city are not in school. In fact, there has been a conspicuous increase in the numbers of vagrant children, boys and girls without schools, jobs, or like Danny, homes of any sort. It's estimated that there are at least three thousand vagrant children in lower Manhattan, most here in the Five Points. Poor tads, they support themselves by selling fruits, nuts, petty merchandise, or just plain scavenging. Even—dare I say it—prostitution. They live on the leavings of this great city. Almost every week there is the gloomy knell of an execution, generally a young man, once one of the street boys.

"And I believe the case for the girls is even worse. Often they are driven to harlotry out of desperation and are murdered or die an early death as a result of disease. How can this happen in Eighteen Forty-seven? It's a disgrace!" She paused, sighing. "You must pardon my vehemence, but I work for the A.I.C.P., and have the statistics at my fingertips."

"Where *is* Danny?" I asked.

"Out back, in our little yard. He's chopping wood. I've had to roast the corn for the girls. Mr. Thorndyke is late. It's after five." She put long, delicate fingers to wide, delicate lips, and flashed large blue eyes at the ceiling. "I usually have more help. The other ladies of the mission would be here, but we have several ill, and several otherwise engaged. We're quite politically active, as you may know. And that reminds me. I'd like to invite you both to attend a Democratic convention tomorrow at three at the Broadway Tabernacle. Afterwards perhaps you'll come to my home. I'm giving a dinner party for a few politicians and friends. We should all be honored, Mr. Poe, if perhaps you would recite a poem or two for us. Of course, you've made a sensation with your 'Raven.'"

"I'd be honored, madam."

# Chapter 23

## SPEAK OF THE DEVIL

Upon our arrival, several Hot Corn Girls had been waiting to receive their wares. Now and again during our conversation others had entered, prepared for work.

Danny Devlin came from the back room carrying a great pile of wood, and heaved it down by the fireplace. He was puffing on a two-inch green butt of cigar.

"*Danny!*" cried Dr. Whitney. "Where did you get that disgusting—*thing*? Take that out of your mouth this instant!"

"Aw, *Jeese!*" cried the boy, removing the soggy cigar.

"Into the fire with it!"

He raised wide thick sandy brows and eyed the morsel wistfully with wide blue eyes.

"I don't know where he gets them," said Dr. Whitney. "This is the third one I've taken from him since you left."

"Have you searched him?" I asked.

"Indeed I have."

We looked back at the boy to discover that he was gone.

"Did he dispose of it?" asked Dr. Whitney.

"We shook our heads, not knowing.

"Girls?"

The Hot Corn Girls looked at us and shrugged.

"And," Dr. Whitney went on, "though I know he does not realize what he is doing, he constantly takes the name of the Lord in vain." She paused, frowning, then smiled largely, and added: "But he *is* adorable, isn't he?"

"You have no children, ma'am?" I asked.

"Unfortunately not. I love children. But I've been an extremely busy woman. College. Post-graduate work in France and Germany. I served my apprenticeship with Dr. Harriet Hunt, of whom you may have heard, in Boston, and have every right to the title 'Doctor,' of which I am extremely proud. Though others may heap scorn and ridicule upon women physicians, our day will come."

Poe stood quite erect, his face pale as paper. I knew he was growing impatient.

"Dr. Whitney," I said, emphasizing the title, "I'd like to question the young ladies."

"Please proceed, then, sir. For as soon as Mr. Thorndyke arrives, he'll have them off on their rounds."

I asked the girls, as a group, if they, any of them, had known Mary Hart at all well. I was told that she had kept to herself.

108

But then one girl stepped forward to say that she had been unusually friendly with the dead girl.

"Your name, please?"

"Sybil O'Shaughnessy, sir."

I asked her to wait after the others had gone.

"But my work, sir."

"I'll pay for the corn out-of-pocket, Miss O'Shaughnessy, and you can take it home early to your family. How's that?"

"Oh, wonderful, sir!"

"This is the end of the season for us," said Dr. Whitney. "You have given Miss O'Shaughnessy a gift of time, Sergeant. I'm sure she thanks you for it."

"Oh, I do, sir! I thank you. And I'll be glad to you tell you anything I know that will be of help."

"Then I thank *you*, Miss O'Shaughnessy," I said. "But first, I'd like to ask *you* a few questions, Dr. Whitney."

"Dr. Whitney," a girl interrupted, "where is Mr. Thorndyke?"

"I don't know, dear," Dr. Whitney said, "but don't bother me just now. I must answer this gentleman's questions. Proceed, sir!"

"Am I correct in assuming that you knew Mary Hart?"

"I don't know if I should say *knew*. I knew her as I know these girls, but, you see, Mr. Thorndyke has direct dealings with the girls generally. I am usually occupied with other missionary matters. Today is quite extraordinary."

"Can you describe her?"

"But you must know what she looked like."

"I don't refer to a physical description. Did you—do you know anything of her personal life?"

"I don't quite see what you're getting at, Sergeant. Of course I know her mother. The ladies of the mission are attempting to relocate Mrs. Hart, to find a home for her. It's difficult to place a blind woman, as you can imagine. We hope, in a few years, to have an institution of some kind—a home for children, the old, and the handicapped—but, at present—"

I interrupted.

"Dr. Whitney, what I am about to ask may seem to you to be—odd. Please, simply answer my next question straight-forwardly."

"Of course. Proceed!"

"Do you remember any contact between Mary Hart and a large man who—who—has no nose . . . eh, wears an artificial nose—?"

"My heavens, no!" She looked askance. "One *does* see so many odd things—and persons—in the Five Points—but no, I should have remembered such a person, I'm confident. But, as I say, I really don't generally deal directly with the girls." She shook her head negatively, pursed her lips, then smiled brilliantly. "I'm afraid not!"

Poe said: "We've discovered, through Mary's mother, that Mary had a brother-in-law named Joe Brody. This Brody was a member of a gang called the Butcher's Gang. You must have seen members of this gang around the Five Points. They're generally quite large men, and accentuate their height by wearing tall plug, or top, hats, which they stuff with soft material and use as helmets. They wear long duster-type coats, and spiked brogans. They're also called Plug Uglies."

"Yes, I've seen them."

"Well, as I say, this Joe Brody, Mary's brother-in-law, was a gang member. Through another member of the gang, we were able to discover that Joe Brody is now known as No-Nose Mullins, the use of the first appellation being self-explanatory."

"In other words," said Dr. Whitney, "you want to learn whether Mary's brother-in-law had been in contact with her."

"Exactly," I said.

"I can't help you there," she said. "I asked Mrs. Hart if she had any relatives and she told me that she did not. I wonder why she told me that."

"Because," said Poe, "she believes Joe Brody is dead."

"I see. But, if Mary had been seeing Joe Brody, wouldn't she have told her mother that he was alive?"

"If Mary had crossed his path," I said, "she would probably think it just as well to let her mother go on believing he was dead. You see, Mary's sister was murdered by the gang five years ago, and Joe Brody disappeared at that time. Mrs. Hart believed him dead, murdered as well."

"How horrible!"

"But Mrs. Hart hated her son-in-law," said Poe. "Mary would not upset her mother by bringing him up—or back from the grave, as it were. As the girls say, Mary was one to keep her own counsel."

"Why was Mary's sister murdered?" asked Dr. Whitney. "And the son-in-law—?"

"Our informer has explained that to us," I said. "It seems that Joe Brody, alias No-Nose Mullins, was threatening to expose a political personage, namely, one Boss Meade—"

"*Mead*!" cried Dr. Whitney.

"You are acquainted with Mr. Meade?" asked Poe.

"More than acquainted. Boss Meade is a member of my party. A Tammany Democrat, but a Democrat, nevertheless. He is to host the convention tomorrow. It's our intention to reform our party, to clean it up, as the gentlemen say. And Boss Meade is our prime target. He is corruption itself!"

"I should be careful, Dr. Whitney," warned Poe, "in any contest with such a man. A Mr. McNeil, a journalist—"

"But, of course," said Dr. Whitney. "I know Russell McNeil. He'll report the convention tomorrow, and will be a guest at my home for dinner. Our reform movement heartily approves the things he has been writing about the Five Points. He's the sort of man we want on our side. How good that you should know him!"

"What is important to understand," I said, "is that Boss Meade was once a butcher, was once a member of the Plug Uglies, and is now *the* butcher of *the* Butcher's Gang. It was this knowledge, I believe, and other, even more incriminating information, that caused the death of Mary's sister, Lucy. Joe Brody threatened to expose Meade. But Meade, not a man to be threatened, retaliated."

"That such a—*brute*—should control the Sixth Ward—*this* ward—or have any political influence at all—or not be in prison—is—horrifying!"

# Chapter 24

## THADEUS THORNDYKE IS LATE

"But where is Mr. Thorndyke? It's getting quite late. Sybil," Dr. Whitney called, "would you be a dear, and run next door to see what's keeping Mr. Thorndyke. He should have been here an hour ago." She turned back to us. "He lives next door on the second floor. Poor man, he's attempting, somehow or other, to become a minister. I suppose it's all part of Andrew Jackson's anti-professionalism. He has no formal training. He's been a concessionaire most of his life, and now his re-birth unto our Savior, I fear, has brought him to poverty through charitable work."

Sybil O'Shaughnessy opened the door and screamed.

# Chapter 25

## THE LATE THADEUS THORNDYKE

Thadeus Thorndyke swayed in the doorway, the windy street behind him, a white patch on his chest, and a cleaver wedged in his skull. He looked about the room imploringly, and pitched forward on his face.

The girls screamed and huddled together. I tried to turn Dr. Whitney away from such horror, but she stood firm. Poe went to the body, gently pushing the frozen Sybil O'Shaughnessy aside. Dr. Whitney took a stride, and went down on one knee beside Thorndyke. She lifted his shoulder and felt his heart. She extracted her hand and felt the neck artery. She looked up at me.

"Dead."

Poe bent over the dead man, pulled a sheet of paper from his chest, and read it. He handed it to me. I read:

> *WARNING REFORMERS!!!*
> *MARY HART WAS #1*
> *THORNDYKE #2*
> *DR. WHITNEY BEWARE!!!*

I pocketed it before Dr. Whitney noticed.

"There's a trail of blood out here," said Poe, from the doorway.

"One of you girls," I said, "run and fetch a leatherhead. Dr. Whitney, do you have the names and addresses of these girls?"

She nodded yes.

"Out you go, then, girls, be off with you. There'll be no work tonight."

Dr. Whitney and I dragged the body into the room to make way at the door for the girls to exit.

She said: "Sergeant, in the backroom you'll find a stack of blankets. Bring one to cover him."

A leatherhead appeared at the door. "What's this?" he said.

"I am Eleanor Whitney, physician. I believe it's obvious what's happened, officer."

"Yes sir—er, uh, *ma'am*."

I threw a blanket across the body. My nerves, which are usually quite steady, had been jangled a bit by the sight of the walking dead man with the cleaver in his head. I was annoyed with myself, especially in the sight of the commanding Dr. Whitney.

Poe had vanished from the door. I stepped out and saw a trail of blood, but no Poe. I called back to the patrolman:

"Where is the girl who fetched you?"

"She went on, sir."

"Terrified, no doubt." It would be difficult to get anything more out of Sybil O'Shaughnessy now. I cursed myself for not having questioned her first.

I followed the bloody trail the few steps to the next door, which was open, and into that house. Dr. Whitney followed me. The blood was on the stairs. I went up, found a door open, and Poe inside. He looked at us, said:

"He was struck at least an hour ago. There's a great deal of blood—some, here, where he must have sprawled, is quite warm—some, over there"—he waved a hand—"quite cold. I should say the blow rendered him unconscious, that after a time he awoke, a living ghost in a nightmare, and found his way to the mission door, probably quite automatically."

"I agree," Dr. Whitney said. "The cleaver prevented him from bleeding to death, staunching the flow."

"Look how the outer ring of blood has not only become cold," said Poe, "—there is a draft here—but it's congealed and darkened." He looked at me. "This might have happened when we were with McNeil, having our lunch," he said.

Downstairs, Dr. Whitney gave the policeman a key to the mission. I left him in charge.

Poe looked ill. Again I suggested that he return to Red Kate's for some much needed sleep. This time he agreed.

117

# Chapter 26

## NO COWARD SOUL IS MINE

Dr. Whitney, Danny Devlin and I rode into the night. Our destination was Dr. Whitney's home in Washington Square. She had kindly offered to keep the boy with her until a place could be found for him.

I let some time pass before telling her the contents of the note. I felt that she had to know, and indeed had every right to know, that she was under such a threat. I was not very surprised to see that the news did not discompose her. I had remarked her courage at the mission, in face of a horror that should have caused most women of her sensitive breeding to faint.

"No coward soul is mine," she replied, apparently quoting someone, when I commented on this. "I have faith, sir, that most women are quite as brave, if not braver, than most men. I have borne a dead child and can bear no other. What more can happen? I have lost a husband who, though considerably older than myself, was to me an object of affection. What more, I pray, sir, can happen? I am in the worldly sense wealthy, but I should be poor in spirit if I allowed the beast who committed such an atrocity upon poor simple Mr. Thorndyke to intimidate me. No, sir. I shall proceed openly tomorrow to my condemnation of that Asmodeus, Boss Meade. I am a worker in the path of righteousness, sir, and I would gladly be a martyr to the cause of good."

"I do not doubt you, ma'am," I said. "But do you give time to other thoughts, at all?"

"What thoughts, Sergeant?"

"Beg pardon, ma'am. Your single-mindedness rather overwhelms me."

"To what, exactly, do you refer, Sergeant? I have a life in society, as well. My dinner party tomorrow, for instance—a reading by Mr. Poe—"

"You no longer wear black?"

"As you see, I do not. My husband, excellent man that he was, has been gone for well over a year. And, as I've said, he was quite my senior."

"You—*loved* him—*greatly*?"

"Loved? In a sense, surely. Sergeant, as you may have noticed, I speak my mind directly. You are not in the company of a lily. Are you asking if we might become friends?"

I cleared my throat, for this was my moment. It was my *destiny*, though I did not know it. "Yes, ma'am. I should like very much to become your friend."

"Then, proceed, Sergeant—proceed, by all means!"

I deposited Dr. Whitney and Danny at the door of her great white house.

"I shall have the house watched," I told her.

"That will be a comfort, Sergeant. I shall look forward to seeing you at the convention. You and Mr. Poe. Is he very ill?"

"Exhausted, I should think. We've had a hectic day."

A butler had opened the door, to my regret. At my back I could hear the stirs of nature in Washington Square Common. The early evening moon beamed down, and a chaos of stars kaleidoscoped overhead. My love wore the faint moon's light like a gossamer wedding gown.

"Eleanor," I said, and took her hand, and kissed it with trembling lips.

# Chapter 27

## ABOUT THE BOSS

Poe and Kate sat at Kate's favored table, where we had sat the night before, when VanBrunt had enjoyed his brief freedom and reunion. They were sipping rum and talking quietly. It wasn't until I took a seat that they became aware of me.

"I've just been telling Kate about what happened at the mission today," said Poe, "and about VanBrunt and the Gimp."

"Thank God Peter's alive!" said Kate. "I'll go to the hospital as soon as possible."

I asked Poe—

"Have you broached the subject yet?"

"I thought I'd wait until you arrived."

"What subject?" asked Kate.

"Your relationship to Boss Meade," I said.

Poe said: "I've noticed that Meade's picture is up in nearly every drinking house in Five Points, along with those of George Washington and Queen Victoria—quite an odd combination, I might remark in passing—but Meade is not to be seen here."

"I'd use it for a dart board," said Kate. "Well, it's no secret, at least as far as I'm concerned. I don't suppose Meade would like me jawing it about, though. Yeah, I knew him—*well*—and *when*. My name is—"

"Katherine Mary Ross," I said.

"From County Kerry," she said proudly. "Meade's real name is Ruark—Patrick Ruark, also from County Kerry. He was a butcher, and a handsome devil. Devil be his name! There was nothing in Ireland for the likes of me and nothing for me here when I came, a snip of a girl, but harlotry. Paddy Ruark—he hadn't changed his name yet—had ambitions. I met him drunk in my bed of business—a brutal, handsome giant. When he learned that I was from Kerry, he offered me an opportunity. *I'll set you up in a green grocery*, he said. *Run me a business*. A green grocery! I was green myself, and didn't know what he meant. But I learned that the green groceries of Paradise Square have got little to do with the few rotting vegetables that sit and stink up the air out front, and all to do with the cheap, poisonous whiskey they sell in back.

"It was in my—or *his*—green grocery that Paddy Ruark formed a gang. The gang was to be his power base and his stepping stone to greater power—of a political sort. Power was all he thought or cared about. He changed his name to one that sounded less Irish, for the really important politics of the city—business, banking, etc.—was firmly in the grasp of the Dutch, English, and Germans. He became Robert Meade, and eventually—you can imagine how—*Boss*

122

Meade." She reached over and took a sip from Poe's glass. His piercing eyes were fixed upon her. "Wirra!" she cried. "But when he went legit, he tossed me aside, calling me nothing but a cat, a whore. A cat I was, perhaps, but not a cheap puss. I bought into a tavern with the money I had made selling bad whiskey, and began to sell good whiskey on the grounds that honesty is the best policy. Now I have this place—tavern and lodging house. Next I'm moving out of Five Points, up to the Bowery, where respectable people go. Maybe Meade wants to become the mayor of New York himself. There's no end to him. But I'll eventually settle for a fancy saloon on Fifth Avenue and the society of bankers." She snorted. "I wanted to marry him once. But if his gang's done this in an effort to frighten the reformers and to make Peter look responsible, I'm going to see McNeil myself, and fill his ears with what I know about Meade. *Boss!* Paddy Ruark, the pig! He feels nothing—least of all for the Irish!"

# Chapter 28

## MULLINS BOUNCES

Mullins stepped up to our table.

"Did you find Max Fisch?" I asked him.

"No. I searched the Old Brewery. All over Paradise Square. I couldn't find him."

"Sit down, Mullins," Poe said. "We have some questions to ask you."

Mullins pulled out a chair and sat down. His eyes seemed to be full of fear and hatred of Poe. Was he jealous because Red Kate appeared to like the poet?

"We have discovered," I said, "that you are—or were— Mary Hart's brother-in-law."

I detected a slight widening of his dull, stupid eyes. Yes, I could imagine him strutting along the infested, swine-ridden streets of the Five Points, a good-looking giant in a leather-stuffed top hat, kicking at the pigs with his hob-nail boots, a cleaver dangling from his belt.

Slowly, he said:

"I was. . ."

"Was what?" I said.

"Was Mary Hart's brother-in-law."

"Why didn't you tell us this before?"

"Because I don't want nothing to do with it. I haven't seen her in five years. She was just a kid, then. The last time I saw Mary, she was but sixteen. I knew her when she was ten. But I haven't laid my eyes on her for five years, I swear! It didn't have nothing to do with me."

"Tell us about Lucy," said Poe. "Tell us how it was that she was murdered with the same type of weapon that was used on Mary."

"I don't know . . ." Like a boy trying to fix his thoughts, Mullins shrugged huge shoulders.

"Tell them," ordered Kate. "And tell me. I like to know who is working for me. Mr. Poe tells me that your real name is Joe Brody. Is that true?"

"My name *is* Joe Brody."

"And you worked for Meade?"

"It was after you and Meade split up, after he opened the American Saloon," he said to Kate. "I heard about you, knew who you were. I was in the Plug Uglies. Lucy took up with Meade behind my back. It must have been going on for about a year before I found out. But it was just then that he was going to ditch her—like he done with you. But Lucy was real smart, smarter than me, and she never let on to

Meade that she was smart. He didn't worry about her at all. She had been with him when he was making deals—"

"What kind of deals?" I asked.

"Deals like using city money to buy land for himself. Lucy was real smart. She had written everything down in a diary."

"Did you see this diary?" asked Poe.

Mullins shook his head. "I never saw it. Look, it was like this. I was drinking with the boys, and they let on about Lucy and Meade. I went home that night and asked her. She was brazen. I never could tell her what to do, on account of she was smarter than me, and I knew it. She could read and write. Then she tells me how Meade's going to do her dirt."

"You weren't angry to find out that your wife was cheating?" I asked.

Again, he shrugged. "We was going our own ways, by then. I wasn't so much angry at her as I was at Meade, making me look—"

"Cuckolding you," said Poe. "Shaming you."

"Anyhow, Lucy says there's a way we both can get even with Meade. I have everything in a diary, she says, names, dates—you go to that reformer, McNeil, and see what he says. So I go and feel McNeil out. He wants evidence."

Poe said: "That's when someone in McNeil's office apparently went to Meade with news of your visit. Meade would have tipsters everywhere."

126

"Then I go home and tell Lucy. We think what to do, how to handle it. We could get a lot of money from Meade, Lucy says, but we have to be careful how we do it. She has the diary stashed away someplace safe, she says. I don't even get to see it until we work things out. Then, on a Sunday morning, we were sitting and thinking what to do, and in breaks a couple of the Butchers. I was pretty drunk from drinking all night. Meade is a bad one, and he's got a hundred like me. So they catch me like that, drunk, and I can't handle them. They search the house, tear everything apart. They ask Lucy about the diary. She says there ain't no diary, that she made it up. But she *could* write one. One cove takes a cleaver to her, and she is down at my feet dead, her head split open. They take me away with them to the backroom of the American Saloon. Meade's waiting there. He asks me where the diary is. I tell him I never saw it. I tell him I don't think there ever was one. I tell him I think Lucy made the whole thing up to calm me down. And because she's angry with him, too. Who knows how a woman's mind works? They beat me a few times, and I say the same things over and over, because it's the truth, I *don't* know.

"Finally, Meade says he believes me. He says Lucy is too dumb to do anything like that, and that I'm even dumber. He tells them to take me out and make me remember not to ever cross him. He tells me never to show my nose in the Five Points again and he fixes it so I don't. I was in the hospital a few days, then I went to work on an oyster sloop, down to Virginia. Stayed down there about a year. When I came back, I didn't look the same. I grew a beard and let my hair grow long. I wanted to stay out of trouble with Meade. I remembered Red Kate. I figured she wasn't no friend of

Meade and neither was I, so I came here and asked for work. She give me it."

"Regarding Mary," Poe said, "who do you think killed her?"

Mullins surveyed the table. "I know you're all on his side, but I figures VanBrunt done it. He said here at the bar that he was going to ask her to marry him. I figures he asks her, and she says no, and, him being drunk, he takes a cleaver to her."

"Where would he get a cleaver?" asked Poe.

"I don't know. Anywhere."

"Why would he take a cleaver with him? He was going to propose marriage."

"Maybe he had it to protect himself on the streets."

"Possibly," said Poe, "but not probably."

"Well," said Mullins, "maybe there *was* a diary, and maybe Mary found it, and maybe Mary and VanBrunt was going to use it to blackmail Meade. . . ."

"An ingenious theory," said Poe, startled by Mullins' capacity for invention, not heretofore observed.

"Yeah," said Mullins, "maybe Mary found it. Maybe Mary and VanBrunt was going to use it the same way Lucy threatened to. But I always figured VanBrunt killed Mary because she wouldn't marry him. I dunno."

Poe said: "Mary's mother said that Mary was prepared to accept VanBrunt's proposal of marriage. You knew he was going to ask her."

"But he was drunk that night. Besides, I didn't know that she would accept him. That's news to me. How could I? I haven't seen her for five years."

"Have you heard of a Mr. Thorndyke?" I asked.

"No."

"You know about the mission? The Association for Improving the Conditions of the Poor?"

"I've heard of it—the reformers?"

"The reformers," said Poe.

"What about the mission? And who's Thorndyke?"

"Thorndyke worked for the mission," said Poe. "He ran the hot corn concession. He was Mary's boss."

"Oh? So what?"

"He was murdered with a cleaver this afternoon," I said.

Mullins shook his head, his ivory beak slowly cutting the green smoke of his cigar. "I don't understand," he said. "What does it mean? What's the connection?" His consternation seemed genuine.

I slapped the warning note on the table and read it to him. *"Mary Hart was number one,"* I read aloud, *"Thorndyke number two. Dr. Whitney, beware!"*

"Who's Dr. Whitney?" he asked.

"One of the ladies of the mission," said Poe.

"A lady doctor?" Mullins looked incredulous. "Well, then," he said, "that explains everything. Maybe it wasn't VanBrunt. No, it wasn't VanBrunt at all. Mary Hart was killed by the gang to scare the reformers."

"You think so?" said Poe. "You certainly leap about in your conclusions, don't you?"

"Well, it's what *you* think, ain't it?"

"I haven't thought things through to any conclusion yet," said Poe. "Have you, Sergeant Goode?"

"No, sir, I haven't," I said. "Mullins, that's all for now."

"Go ahead," said Kate to Mullins. "We'll settle accounts later." She looked at Mullins as he stood, tilting her head toward the bar. "Bring up another case of the good stuff," she said, "we're swamped tonight."

"Yes, ma'am," he said, and ambled off, into the crowd.

The Emerald Isle was packed. A contingent of Portuguese sailors, in that afternoon, added a boisterous festiveness to the din.

# Chapter 29

## MIDNIGHT CONFIDENCES

"What do you intend to do about Mullins?" Poe asked Red Kate.

"He came to me because I'm against Meade," she said. "Why should I turn him out?"

"Indeed," said Poe, noncommittally.

I looked at Poe's haggard face and said, "Let's turn in."

He nodded agreement.

"Goodnight, Kate," I said, rising.

"Goodnight, gentlemen." We left her sitting in deep thought.

When we came to Poe's room, he drew me in, closed the door, and offered me the one chair in the room. He sat on the bed.

"Well, Sergeant, what do you think?"

"There's really only one thing I feel sure of, that is that everything we've learned today points away from Mr. VanBrunt."

"I agree. You have observed the contradictions, of course. If we are to take at face value the note left by Thorndyke's murderer—then how account for the strangulation of the Gimp?"

"I wonder," I said, "if there really was—is—a diary?"

"If there is such a diary, it would have to be in the possession of Mary Hart's mother. That little family would seem to have had no friends."

"But surely she would have turned the diary over to the police—or to someone who could make use of it."

"Perhaps not. Consider—the diary was probably morally, maybe legally, incriminating to Lucy. If such a diary existed, it would be, after all, a record of Lucy's moral turpitude—a diary of adultery, debauchery and projected blackmail. The impoverished old lady remains a highly moral woman. She would not want the diary made public. Then, too, consider that she's blind. It could be that the diary is somewhere about and she knows nothing of it."

"It must have occurred to you," I said, "that Mullins, knowing the value of such an item, would have searched for it. He must have had opportunity."

"And we should certainly have seen the results. Had Mullins laid hands on the diary, it would have become apparent—to wit, he would not now be working for Kate, but would either be rich, relatively, or dead. No, Mullins doesn't have it."

Poe furrowed his high, wide brow. "But did Mullins have the opportunity? Did anyone, without causing notice? Had

132

Mrs. Hart been broken in upon, she would have said. Her place is too small to have been burgled while she was there, and her not know, and she claims never to leave it."

"Except for church services—at the mission, on Sunday morning."

"All right," said Poe, "suppose someone—Meade, say, or his agents—broke in on a Sunday morning and got the diary—"

Poe got up wearily from the bed and pulled out a bottle of rum from the dresser drawer. He sat down again and poured two glasses. He handed me one and raised his to me. *Sante!*"

"Cheerio!" I replied, and drank. "No use trying to use Mullins's word against Meade. Mullins is not a good witness. His character is bad, and five years have elapsed. It's quite frustrating for a policeman. I should have arrested those thugs back at the fortification, but I couldn't. If we had marched them out at gunpoint, we'd have been mobbed. Had I sent a detachment of police back in, there'd have been a riot. I hope someday to see an adequate police force in this city."

"Have you read Vidocq?"

"No, sir—I haven't. Who is he?"

"Please call me Eddie, Sergeant, as all my friends do."

"Then let me be Jon to you—Eddie."

"Well done. Vidocq was a French police spy, whose memoirs ran in serial form in a journal—oh, sometime ago. I found them fascinating. Indeed, they suggested certain aspects of my story, 'Murders in the Rue Morgue.' I should think that you would enjoy reading them."

"I shall seek them out," I said.

Poe refilled our glasses.

"Why did you become a policeman—*Jon*?"

"I was reared on rectitude—*Eddie*. My father was owner-master of a ninety-ton schooner. He brought oysters up from the sea islands of the coast of North Carolina and carried back miscellaneous freights to Southern ports. As a boy, I made many trips with him, and so learned something about sea life.

"In Eighteen-Forty, his schooner sank in a storm off Long Island. All aboard were drowned, including my mother, who had sailed for pleasure. I was not aboard because of a mild but disabling illness, and was recuperating with an aunt. I was left penniless. I am still waiting for an insurance settlement.

"In Forty-five, I went on the revenue steamer 'Morgan' and remained with her for several months. I remember the great fire in New York of that year, at which the crew of the 'Morgan' and a contingent of United States Marines from the Brooklyn Navy Yard assisted as guardians of property. That was my first experience as a keeper of the peace.

"I grew weary of life at sea, left the 'Morgan,' took up residence in Greenwich Village, and went into business, selling products brought to Washington Market by the river craft. In spring, summer, and fall I was kept busy, but during the winter months I had nothing to do. I had never thought of police work until my cousin asked me if I'd like to take his place. As you can see, I am three-quarters of me bulk—"

"Burly muscle, Jon!"

"In any case, made for action."

"Hence, the police." Poe seemed to be thinking back. "I was not always as you see me today," he said. "As a young man, I was an athlete. I still hold the broadjump record for the University of Virginia."

"Yes, Mr. VanBrunt told me that—and that you were a soldier—an enlisted man."

"Yes—before I went to West Point. Back in May of Eighteen Twenty-seven—about twenty years ago now—I enlisted in the army under the name of Edgar A. Perry. I rose to the rank of Sergeant Major in nine months— something of a record, I believe. I was in for two years. . ."

"I became a police sergeant in about the same length of time."

"The two good Sergeants," said Poe, toasting us with raised glass.

"To the two good Sergeants!" I said.

We drank, and fell into an embarrassed silence, which I finally broke by saying:

"You comported yourself like a soldier today, Eddie."

"Ah, physical courage is nothing, particularly to one in my melancholy state of mind. But I don't know if I have emotional courage enough. The thought of my lost young wife fairly kills me, Jon."

"You may have saved my life."

Poe shrugged. "A worthy life. You are a bachelor?"

"I've never had time for women. But now that I've been promoted, I'd like to marry and have children. I am studying law, thinking of the future. I've been living meagerly, saving my money."

"Money," said Poe, "or the lack of it, has been the curse of my life. Had I the money to pay for good medical treatment—had I the money to buy decent food—had I the money for *blankets*—my darling might still grace the world."

"Was there no way?"

"I *worked*—harder than ten men. And not only in journalism and literature. I have laid bricks. I have clerked. I have done menial labor. Money will simply have nothing to do with me. Oh, I am the wrong man for this commercial world!"

"Perhaps too good for it, Eddie."

He placed his gray eyes upon me.

"You've made me feel better, Jon. Not in that last com-
ment—I am none too good for this world, I assure you. But,
you see, since my wife died, I have been . . . well . . . as you
found me. Spiritually ill. Oh, rot! I've been drinking, and I
have no tolerance for the stuff. I even dislike the taste of it,
so I throw it down in a gulp. I want the result—
forgetfulness. But seeing Peter has reminded me of my
youth, when all was new and shining. And Peter, too, is the
victim of circumstances. I have felt myself to be a victim of
circumstances. But, no, the fault is not in our stars, but in
ourselves. By allowing me to work with you, you have
given me purpose. It gives me life again—instead of the
gaping abyss between myself and my darling Virginia. It
gives me an opportunity to return the gift of friendship
which I owe Peter—and you as well, Jon. It gives me a
problem to solve. I can forget myself in this pursuit as I can
only do otherwise in the nothingness of total comatose inebriation."

The sky was beginning to lighten when we drained the
bottle.

Poe finally appeared calm.

"Jon," he said, "perhaps we should get some sleep."

## Chapter 30

## APPETITES

I arose at nine, fetched Poe, and had him packed aboard a carriage before he was fully awake.

"I'm concerned about your health, Eddie," I said. "I'm taking you to my boarding house in Greenwich Village. There's no better breakfast to be had in Manhattan Island."

It was true. My landlady took great pride in being able to set before her boarders excellent and bountiful meals. Her boarders came from all over Europe—there was a Russian cap-maker, a German cabinet-maker, a shoemaker from Denmark, a clothier from Poland, a lamp-maker from England, and, from Ireland, an actor—Kevin O'Connell.

I said: "Afterward we'll get a change of clothes for you. Remember Kevin, at the fire? I think he's just about your size, don't you? I know he'll help us with the haberdashery. We must look good for Dr. Whitney at the convention this afternoon."

"Ah, yes," said Poe, at last waking up. "Today we attend the convention. I don't care too much for politics, but it should prove interesting. Besides, I believe Meade will be speaking. I'd like to get a look at him."

"Have you any appetite, Eddie?"

"I believe I have. Yes, by Gad, I am famished!"

"You've eaten like a bird since we met. A good meal will give you strength—and health. I myself have an enormous appetite—at all times."

## Chapter 31

## A GHOST ON GREENWICH STREET

We pulled to the curb in front of 130 Greenwich Street. Poe got out, and then it was as if he had been struck by an arctic wind, and frozen in his tracks.

"What is it?" I asked.

"This house. A grim coincidence. I stayed here once. It was the spring of Forty-four. I'd decided to come back to New York after living for a time in Philadelphia, where things had gone bad again. I brought Virginia with me. We had to leave my mother-in-law, Mrs. Clemm, behind in Philadelphia, until we had money to send for her and our cat, Caterina. We were directed to this house, as being reasonable, warm, and serving good food. I had about four dollars and fifty cents in my pocket. We ate an enormous, delicious breakfast. One of the best meals I've ever had. I wrote my 'Balloon Hoax' while we were here, to make some quick money. We were so happy then, though we were awfully poor. But Virginia wasn't coughing. She'd improved so much. We thought—we hoped—"

"Come," I said, "let's get in."

Poe followed me upstairs. I knocked at Kevin O'Connell's door.

"Ah, good morning, Sergeant, and Mr. Poe," said the actor, smiling. "What a pleasant surprise!"

"'Morning, Kevin," I said. "Do you suppose you could provide Mr. Poe with a change of clothes?"

"I live out at Fordham," said Poe, "and we've been invited to attend a Democratic convention today and a dinner party this evening. I need some refurbishing."

"Certainly, certainly, Mr. Poe. Come in. We'll see what I have. The shirt off me back is none too much for the man who saved me miserable life to ask of me."

No sooner had Poe stepped over the threshold than he sighed, "Oh, Jon this is the very room!"

He looked so shaken that I said: "Kevin, we'll go on to my room, if you don't mind. Would you be so good as to bring over whatever you think appropriate. And please bring some of your actors' makeup. I'm going to remove these bandages. My bruised hide will have to do. We'll be in your debt. I think Eddie needs to rest a bit and have something to eat. He's a little under the weather."

"Of course, Jon. Pleasure to do so."

By now Poe had eased into the room. He looked about, trance-like. "Oh. . ." he moaned—"Oh, Virginia, Sissy, what are you doing here?" He turned to us. "Gentlemen, this is my wife, Virginia. I call her Sissy because she is like a sweet sister to me. Have you ever seen anyone so beautiful? I bid you look upon her fawn-like eyes and into the mystery of life. O dark, dark eyes. I assure you, gentlemen, that she is the gentlest of creatures. But don't look, don't look at the blood on her blouse. She was singing and the blood erupted. It has spoiled her blouse. How have you come to be here, Virginia? Were you waiting for me, your Eddie? Oh my darling, my darling!"

"He's hallucinating," said Kevin. "I've seen a lot of it. We'll pour a drink down his throat. That's what he needs." Kevin got a bottle of Irish whiskey and almost force-fed Poe a drink, holding his head with one hand and the glass with the other. "Come along now, old fellow. Drink this. You'll be all right."

Poe shuddered, and said, "Yes. Yes, that's better. Where did she go?"

"Into heaven, dear fellow. Your bride went into heaven, no doubt of it."

"Yes, yes," said Poe. "Thank you. Thank you. I saw her though, as plain as day, I tell you. But of course—that's impossible, isn't it?" He looked at the half-empty glass and drained it. "It must have been the effect of the laudanum," he said. "But it was so real."

# Chapter 32

## WEAK AND WEARY

In dark melancholy, Poe sat in my great armchair, gazing out the window onto the street below. Ten or fifteen minutes passed while I filled the wash basin and cleaned myself up and shaved. I removed the bandages and covered my abrasions with Kevin's stage makeup.

"You know, Jon," he said, "this has been a shock to me. As I told you last night, working with you has distracted me from my troubles. But just when I begin to think that I might pass one day without being reminded that Virginia is gone to me forever, something brings it all back and I feel . . . *struck* again."

"I know it must be very hard for you, Eddie. You must have been very happy with such a companion."

"She gave me the one bit of light I've found in this dismal place, Jon." It was clear that he meant the world.

I was combing my hair when Kevin knocked at the door and handed me a dark, clean suit and linen. "I think these will do," he said. "If you need anything, just let me know."

Poe washed and dressed and we went down to breakfast. Most of the tenants had already eaten and gone. We had the dining room to ourselves.

Breakfast was hot, strong coffee, veal cutlets, ham and fresh eggs, delicious bread and butter, and a bowl of fruit.

"It is all the same as it was that morning," said Poe, "only now it is all different."

"Will you eat, Eddie?" I said, passing him a platter of cutlets.

"Only coffee," he said, "and maybe an apple."

## Chapter 33

## KATE'S WRATH

Visiting hours at the City Hospital were between ten and noon. We expected to find Red Kate among the visitors. Mullins was with her. They had just come from seeing VanBrunt.

"He hasn't regained consciousness," Kate told us. "The doctor says he could be hemorrhaging inside of his head. They might have to operate. You know, he hasn't been in good health, drinking and all. He might *die!*"

She fell into Poe's arms.

"I'll kill whoever did this to him," she said. "I'll have their ears!"

"You've been a good friend to Peter," said Poe, "and I count you as my friend as well, so I feel that I can say this without incurring your wrath, Kate. But, terrible as you would like to sound, you do not take ears—your heart is too soft under your bluster."

"What?" said Kate, tears streaming down her cheeks, making rivulets in her paint. "What do you mean, Eddie?"

"I mean that you have a jar filled with wax ears behind your bar. You are more bark than *bite*, my dear."

"Oh—Eddie—"

Poe patted her gently on the back, until her tears subsided.

"I heard tell of Max Fisch," said Mullins, Kate's vademe-cum.

"Where? How?"

"Some cove told me he saw Max in a diving bell in the Five Points."

"When?" I asked.

"When did he see him or when did he tell me, you mean?"

"Blast it man! When did he see him?"

"Last night. Told me this morning. I went over to the place, but nobody there remembers him."

"Is your informant reliable?"

"If he says he saw Max Fisch, he saw Max Fisch."

Kate said:

"We saw Boodle Coign before."

"How is he?" I asked.

"He was on his way out," said Mullins. "I don't know him, but Kate does."

"He used to come in my place once in a while," said Kate. "I never liked him. I don't like having Plug Uglies with their top hats knocking at my candles and their spiked brogans digging up my floor. They remind me of Meade when he was young, and they all work for him one way or another." She was standing alone now, wiping her eyes. "Looks like his friends took an ear from Coign," she added, "and not a wax one, judging by the blood on the bandage."

"I think he'll be leaving town," said Mullins, "the way I did five years ago. When they do this to you"—he touched his ivory nose—"or this"—he touched an ear—"it means that you better leave town for a while."

"If Meade is behind what has happened to Peter," said Kate, "I'm going to McNeil and tell him everything I know about Meade's past. It might not ruin him down in Five Points, but it'll hurt him with his rich uptown connections."

"Meade must be behind it," said Mullins.

"At least some of it," I said. I turned to Poe, but he was gone. "Where did Poe go?" I asked.

"Down the hall," said Mullins.

"I'm going to McNeil in any case," said Kate. "I've owed Meade ever since he threw me over like I was a sack of chew. I've made up my mind, I'm going to McNeil."

Kate strode out with Mullins behind her. I went looking for Poe.

# Chapter 34

## LAUDANUM

Down the hall were several doors. I looked in each and went on, coming finally upon one marked *Laboratory*. Poe was inside, sitting among vials and test tubes, sipping some kind of concoction.

"What have you there?" I asked.

"Forgive me, Jon," he said.

"What is it?"

"Laudanum," he said. "Everywhere I turn, I am haunted by Virginia's spirit. I would not be able to go on with you, without this, the only balm in Gilead."

I went with Poe to a nearby tavern, where he had several drinks while I smoked a cigar. He told me of the hemorrhages his Virginia had suffered:

"Each time it was as if she had died, and then each time she would grow stronger, so that there was hope—hope only to be dashed again."

At last I was able to get him into a hack, and we were on our way. It was nearly three.

# Chapter 35

## J'ACCUSE!

At Anthony Street and Broadway, a crowd flowed into the Broadway Tabernacle. This great, domed Congregationalist Church was often used for public meetings. Inside, a banner proclaimed a convention of Manhattan Democrats, hosted by Alderman Meade of the Sixth Ward.

I saw Dr. Whitney up front, by the rostrum. She was with the reform mayoral candidate, Fleetwood O'Brien, and several other ladies and gentlemen. I saw Wilson, the patrolman I had appointed to protect her.

"Dear lady," I said in greeting.

"Sergeant Goode, Mr. Poe. How fine you both look!"

"I do not *feel* fine, madam," said Poe. He was a bit glassy-eyed.

"I am sorry to hear it, sir."

"Mr. Poe has had a shock," I said. "An unhappy coincidence. He'll be all right. I'm happy to find you safe and sound—"

"Call me *Eleanor* . . . Jon."

"Eleanor."

149

"Have you met Mr. O'Brien?"

"I have not had the pleasure, but I've seen his campaign posters. Sir," I said, shaking his hand, "it is my intention to vote for you."

"Well done, Sergeant," said Fleetwood O'Brien, a wide-eyed, open-faced, middle-sized man with black hair parted down the center and black mustaches that separated when he smiled. "Mr. Poe, I am an admirer of your work. Your 'Raven' has become the talk of the town."

"Mr. O'Brien," said Poe, taking the politician's hand, "I wrote a story called 'The Gold Bug' that won me a prize and my first notice, but the bird has beaten the bug all hollow. Would you mind explaining the political situation to me?"

"Certainly," said the handsome reform candidate. "The Democratic Party in Manhattan is divided into several factions, only two of which are of real importance. They are Tammany and the Reform Democrats. Dr. Whitney and I are fighting for reform, to wrest control of the party from Tammany Hall, the sachems of which have used their power for their own benefit, for self-aggrandizement and personal gain. They are corruption itself. Through demagoguery they win the votes of the poor, and then keep their power by keeping the poor down, to make use of, to begin the whole process again. I only wish Dr. Whitney were able to run for mayor. She is, as it were, the better man."

"I'm sorry, sir," said Poe, "but we Southerners are unused to women in politics. Or in medicine. But Dr. Whitney has inspired the germ of a story in me."

"Dear Mr. Poe," Eleanor broke in, "I'm afraid that women in politics is a fact that you must become accustomed to. It won't be long before women have the vote, I can assure you. I am in contact with some very forceful ladies at this moment—Lucretia Mott and Elizabeth Cady Stanton, to name a couple—and we shall be convening in Seneca Falls, New York, next year with several hundred women of like mind to consider the most expeditious ways to accomplish that goal. There'll be no stopping us!"

"I commend you, madam—*Doctor*," said Poe, bowing slightly and smiling.

How I admired my Eleanor!

"*Quiet!*" cried a ward-heeler. "Quiet, please! It's now my happy duty to introduce the man who has made the Sixth Ward what it is today—a defender of the poor and downtrodden, a defender of our great red, white, and blue against all who would attempt to lower it, especially the English—a man of the people, a self-made man, a man who has pulled himself up by his own bootstraps, a man who seen his opportunities and took 'em—former State Senator, Assemblyman, High Sachem of Tammany, Sixth Ward Chief of the Volunteer Red Dragon Hook & Ladder, Police Magistrate, County Supervisor, and our Alderman—Boss Meade!"

None in our company applauded.

"Another Goliath," said Poe in my ear.

Indeed, physically, Meade was a giant, one of the breed of Mullins and Boodle Coign, one of the type of the Plug Ugly. But the "ugly" in Plug Ugly referred to disposition rather

151

than, necessarily, looks. Meade was a dark, handsome man, of the type called black Irish. He looked to be in his forties.

He said:

"There are those who would take our beloved Sixth Ward— our beloved Paradise Square—our beloved Five Points— and turn it into a playground for the rich! And how would they do this? Would they make rich the poor and downtrodden of Five Points? No! They would throw them into the streets, out of the only homes they know. They would throw them into the streets, I say, and let them freeze. They would let them freeze, but not in Five Points, not where they would instate the rich, personages with names like Whitney, Astor and Grinnell. Such people would not have the likes of *us* underfoot. We are trash to be swept up by the broom of wealth.

"When the reformers say that they want to clean up Five Points, what do they mean? Throw the poor out of the only homes they have?

"Look at the Old Brewery. Now, I'll give you that it's a hell hole. But it's the only place those poor folks have to live in. Where would they go, if they were turned out? Could they set up camp on the lawns of the rich reformers of the 15th Ward, across the street from Washington Square—or in Washington Square itself? *No!* Then let the rich nativist English and Dutch reformers of *Washington* Square leave hands off the poor of *Paradise* Square. In the 15th Ward a population almost exactly as large as that of the 6th Ward lives on three times as much space, and they own the poor tenements of the Five Points, to boot. Reform? Let the rich and greedy landowners reform themselves—"

Eleanor shouted: "You don't want the Five Points changed because it's your power base. Make the 6th Ward *clean*, and who would you find there to support you?"

Fleetwood O'Brien shouted: "Meade, you demagogue! You know perfectly well that it is our intention to construct new, inexpensive housing for those poor unfortunates! And my name is not Astor, but O'Brien."

"You've probably changed it!" cried Meade.

"You *have* changed yours!" cried O'Brien.

"Back off," said Meade, "or I'll not be responsible for the patriotic wrath of the crowd."

Several black top-hats came floating across the heads around us.

"We will not succumb to your terror tactics!" cried Eleanor.

"Terrorist, am I?" said Meade. "What terror?"

"The murder of the Hot Corn Girl!"

"You had better speak to your lawyer, Dr. Whitney," said Meade, "before you repeat such a black lie as that."

"Mr. O'Brien *is* my lawyer. And what about the murder of Mr. Thadeus Thorndyke?"

"Now who, in the name of sweet Jesus, is Mr. Thorndyke?"

"You know perfectly well who he was. You had him killed—along with Mary Hart—to frighten us, the reformers, who will unseat you and your whole corrupt pack of wolves if it's the last thing we do. You are a disgrace to the Democratic Party, which my husband helped to found in Eighteen Twenty-three, before you came to our beloved country, probably. You are, indeed, a disgrace to America, and a disgrace to Ireland as well!"

"I'll not be responsible for the just wrath of this crowd," cried Meade, and the top hats floated above the heads of the audience, towards us, with new speed.

"Back out!" I said, taking Eleanor's arm.

"I'll stand my ground," she cried.

"Not here and now," I said, and pulled her back through the crowd, toward the door.

"Unhand me, sir," she said.

"I would do anything for you, Eleanor, my dear, but that," I replied, and fairly dragged her back toward the door. Suddenly a Plug Ugly loomed before me. I drew my pistol. "Back now," I said, and he slowed his advance. I looked for Poe, Fleetwood O'Brien, my policeman, and the others. They were retreating apace. Wilson held his pistol at the ready.

We boarded carriages on Broadway and hastily departed the environs of the Broadway Tabernacle.

"You have disgraced me," said Eleanor to me.

154

"On the contrary," said Poe. "He's behaved wisely, gallantly."

"Indeed, Eleanor," said Fleetwood O'Brien. "I'm very glad that the Sergeant was present."

"Let's call it a tactical withdrawal," I said.

She was a bit mollified, but still angry. I sought to change the subject. "Have you ladies of the mission found a place for Mrs. Hart, yet?"

"Indeed, we have. With the help of several of our ladies, she's been packing. She'll be leaving tomorrow to take up residence at the Fifth Avenue Home for the Aged."

"You say she's packed?" asked Poe.

"Well, what few things she has . . . a suitcase, a few boxes, a steamer trunk."

"Would you mind taking us to Mrs. Hart's?"

"What? Now?"

Poe looked at me. "Let's have a look at her possessions, Sergeant."

I nodded in agreement. "We'll see you tonight, at eight. Mr. O'Brien, you and patrolman Wilson please keep a sharp eye on Dr. Whitney, won't you?"

As Poe and I exited the carriage before Mrs. Hart's tenement, Eleanor said: "I wish I could go in with you, but I have so much to do before this evening, and I need some time to compose myself. The convention was a fiasco."

"Wilson," I called up, "keep close watch till I arrive at Dr. Whitney's."

I turned to Poe. "The diary?" I said.

"The diary," Poe repeated, rapping gently upon Mrs. Hart's window.

# Chapter 36

## NONE SO BLIND

The unseasonably warm weather had vanished and now the November dusk brought the threat of snow. Scudding dark clouds overhead: evening coming on.

"We had better not tell Mrs. Hart that Joe Brody is alive," Poe said. "We would only have to explain the rest to her, and add to her miseries. But, if we get a resolution to this business, and, with it, justice—"

Mrs. Hart opened the door. "Who is it?" she said.

"Sergeant Goode," I said, "and Mr. Poe. May we come in?"

"Oh, yes, Sergeant. I recognize your lovely deep voice."

"May I suggest," said Poe, "with the kindliest intentions, madam, that you enquire as to who is outside your door before opening it?"

"And that soft Southern accent, Mr. Poe—I would recognize your voice anywhere, as well. But I have no fear. What should I be afraid of? I am ill, old, blind, and alone in the world. If I were killed, what matter? But who would bother to harm me? I only wish I could trade my life for the lives of my daughters, but death would have the valuable and leave the worthless."

"There is no trading in immortal souls," said Poe. "Each is all, madam. Death is random and, in the aspect of eternity, fair. Only by human standards does death appear stupid."

"Come in, please, Mr. Poe—Sergeant. I would offer you tea, but, as you can see, all my things are packed. I am being sent off to an institution."

"It's about your things that we have come," I said.

"To pick them up?"

"No, ma'am. We'd like to have a look through them, if we might."

"But they are all packed. The ladies of the mission packed them—"

"Yes, ma'am."

"But I don't understand. What can you want to look through my things for?" She stepped backward against a chair and sat down, clutching her Bible, her knuckles white.

"We believe that there could be something among your things of which you are unaware," said Poe.

"How can that be? I have so little. I touched most of the things as they were being packed—to see if I wanted to keep them."

"But something could have eluded you," I said. "May we look for ourselves?"

"Will it help in finding out who killed Mary?"

"We think so," I said.

"Then, go ahead. But you will repack them as you go, won't you?"

"Indeed," I said.

There were two valises, one leather and one of cloth, several boxes, tied with string, and a steamer trunk.

Poe already had one of the boxes open and was going through its contents, unwrapping and rewrapping as he went. I fell to with him.

We ignored anything too small to contain our conception of a diary-shaped object, but looked into larger pots, folders, and other such that might contain it.

"What is it exactly that you are looking for?" asked Mrs. Hart.

"Papers, letters, a book," I said, working.

"But how would I have come by anything that would interest you?"

"One of your daughters could have placed it among your things," I said. "Most probably Lucy."

"Lucy? Then it would have been put here over five years ago."

"Most probably," I said. "If at all."

"What would it be about?"

Poe and I exchanged glances. I said:

"We're uncertain."

"Uncertain? But—"

"This trunk is padlocked," said Poe.

"I haven't opened it in years," said Mrs. Hart. "It contains only a few precious things from my girlhood."

"You haven't examined those things for some time, then," said Poe. "Have you the key?"

"Yes, but . . . must you?"

"Did Lucy or Mary have access to the key?" asked Poe.

"Yes. I keep it here, pressed in my Bible. But those things are only memories of a happier youth."

"If we do not look, we shall not have done what must be done," said Poe, "in order to find whoever is responsible for Mary's death."

"Very well, then." Mrs. Hart resolutely fingered the pages of her Bible and extended the key into space. I took it and opened the trunk.

"Ah!" sighed Poe, at the sight of some dusty crushed flowers. He pushed them onto a piece of paper and placed them gently on the floor beside the trunk. "We shall be *very* careful, *very* delicate," he said.

I looked at the silent old lady, whose blind, shrunken eyes were welling with tears. Not much luck for some, I thought.

"Look," said Poe. "Wait. What's this?"

"A Bible," I said.

"A Bible?" said Mrs. Hart. "But—"

"Don't you see?" said Poe. "Look at the inscription."

It was inscribed by Lucy Brody, to her mother. I couldn't understand why Poe was so excited. It was just an old, coverless Bible.

Poe turned to Mrs. Hart. "The same size. May I see your Bible, Mrs. Hart?"

"My Bible?"

"I believe I've found your Bible—the *true* holy writ."

"But I have it here."

"No, madam, I believe you have something else there, with the cover of your Bible concealing it."

Mrs. Hart confusedly handed Poe her Bible, which he flipped open under my eyes.

161

"What is it?" asked Mrs. Hart, deeply agitated.

"Your daughter's diary," I said. "You've been carrying it with you for five years, thinking it your Bible. The diary itself has been filled in with blank pages to bring it to the proper size, then glued into the Bible cover."

"Lucy did it," said Poe, "probably just before she was murdered. She knew that it would never be out of your hands, that you would let no one but herself read it to you, as you promised."

"But how," said Mrs. Hart. "When?"

"When she was compelled to," said Poe, looking at me. "I should think quite soon after she fell out with Meade, or sensed such a falling out in the wind."

"Who's Meade?" asked Mrs. Hart. "The political person?"

"No, no. Not that Meade. This one is a figure of minor importance to the case," said Poe, hastily. "He's of no concern to you, dear madam, I assure you." He paused. "When did you see Lucy last?"

"The Friday of the week-end she was killed. It's so vivid. Strange, I can't remember what happened last week, but I remember the last time I was with Lucy as if it were a moment ago."

Poe looked grim. He said: "I can understand that."

Mrs. Hart went on: "She spent the whole day with me reading . . ."

"That's it!" said Poe, excitedly. "I should surmise that while she was here that day she must have transferred the diary to the Bible cover. Did you perhaps take a nap, that day?"

"Why, yes, I slept for an hour or so and was surprised to find Lucy still here when I awoke. I thought how sweet and thoughtful it was of her to have stayed."

Poe pointed toward the screen with the bed behind it. "You were asleep behind the screen," he put the flat of his hand on the table, "and Lucy sat *here* and did her work with glue. The key to the chest was in the Bible. She took your Bible and put it in the chest and put the key back in her newly bound diary. She didn't remove the Bible from the room because it meant too much to both of you. She put it with your treasurers. She knew that the diary would never leave your hands, nor that you would allow anyone else to read from it, including Mary. It is as it was in my story, 'The Purloined Letter.' Mrs. Hart has been waving the diary under our very noses. Indeed, under her own, without knowing it."

Mrs. Hart said: "But something else comes to mind. I remember now that I discovered that the lock was broken the week after Lucy's death. I remember because I had to replace it. If she had the key and opened it with the key, why did she break the lock?"

"Joe Brody broke the lock," said Poe. "Searching for the diary."

163

"Then he must have seen the Bible in the trunk," I said.

"Yes," Poe said, "but it didn't mean anything to him. Why should it? He probably didn't even know that Lucy had ever given her mother a Bible. While on the other hand it was precisely what we were looking for."

"But when you first showed it to me," I said, "it didn't mean anything to me either."

"It would have, in only a second, Jon."

Poe hastily repacked the trunk, and locked it, giving the key to Mrs. Hart. He worked abstractedly while I read an entry from the diary.

"It's a gold mine," I said.

"What does she say?" ask Mrs. Hart. "Oh, I'm so confused!"

"Forgive me, ma'am," I said, "but I cannot disclose the contents."

"But, Sergeant . . . Does she mention me?"

"You see," said Poe, "Lucy had some important information pertaining to criminal activity, to which she had been witness. It was her intention to help the police."

"And that was why she was killed? But what about Mary?"

"We don't know yet," I said. Indeed, my mind was racing like a mill-wheel at spring thaw. I saw part—and parts—a vague pattern with great gaps. I wondered if Poe's imagination could fill them in, and, as if on cue, Poe said:

"I think I can imagine what happened here."

"Would you care to clarify?"

"I cannot until the whole crystallizes."

"Well," I said, "I must get this diary to my superiors."

We completed the task of repacking Mrs. Hart's possessions, and stood before her, neither of us wishing to leave the old blind woman in such an agitated state.

"We'll take both books," Poe said, "with your permission, madam, and have your Bible rebound for you. I'll see to it myself, and return it to you by my own hand."

"Can we do anything more for you—*now*?" I said.

The old lady shook her head, then bethought herself.

"The big Bible on the stand. Mary used to read to me from it; but I told you that, didn't I? Would you bring it here to me, by my side, where I can touch it?"

I moved the Bible and stand from among her possessions, to her side.

"You will bring my dear Lucy's Bible back quickly, Mr. Poe? I feel lost without it."

"I promise you, madam."

"We'll stop at the mission," I said, "and ask if one of the ladies can come over to pay you a visit."

"I'll locate you through Dr. Whitney," said Poe.

"Yes. Very well, then. I thank you both. You've been very kind."

Outside, I told Poe: "I feel like a swine."

"What were we to do?" he asked gloomily. "We had to find the diary, if it existed, and we certainly couldn't tell her the nature of it. She's suffered enough. Should we have told her that her daughter was married to one vicious criminal and consorting with another?"

"Her faith is her strength," I said.

"Yes—or do we delude ourselves?" said Poe bitterly.

# Chapter 37

## HEADQUARTERS

En route to Headquarters we read the diary. It recorded the events of a year. It was highly selective, detailed, and deeply incriminating of Boss Meade. Captain Henchard and others at Anthony Street were implicated.

"If any of this can be confirmed," I said, "it'll rock Meade from power. Indeed, it'll put him behind bars."

"That will be a service," said Poe. "But I feel that we have taken a wrong turn at a fork in the road."

Police Headquarters for the City of New York was located in the basement of City Hall. There I learned that Meade had put pressure on Chief Matsell to have me taken off the case, or perhaps even off the force, as some had it. But he had had no success because others in high places wanted me to continue the investigation. I worked for some time analyzing the diary with several inspectors and City Hall politicos, while Poe, who knew about such things, went to a local bookbinder to have the Bible rebound. He rejoined me an hour later, smelling a bit of rum, and we went on to Washington Square.

# Chapter 38

## A GALA NIGHT

Our cab reined in behind a magnificent carriage with red wheels and tongue and green body. The black coachman's livery was blue and silver, and the harness of the white horses was mounted with gold. Several richly dressed ladies and gentlemen alighted from the vehicle. We followed them up the steps. Eleanor greeted us at the door. Behind her the official greeter, the butler, stood in annoyed dignity.

The ladies ahead of us were resplendent in silk, lace, diamonds, and furs. But Eleanor, who was simply clad in a deep-blue velvet gown, a strand of lustrous pears about her neck, out shown them all.

"Gentlemen," she said. "I'm so glad to have you both back. Almost everyone has arrived. Come in, there are a few people I especially want you to meet and a few you already know."

Poe stepped forward and took her hand. He held it for a moment and then passed on into the house.

She gave me her arm and we joined the other guests.

"Poe and I have some exciting news. I'll tell you about it when we have a moment."

"Jonathan, I don't know what I'd do without you. Fleetwood has been telling me that I behaved a bit rashly this afternoon. But I cannot keep silent in the face of such a scoundrel as Meade. And this gathering is not entirely to my liking, either. Most of the guests are associates of my late husband and they've done nothing to earn their wealth but sit on urban land, and watch the rapid appreciation of land values that comes with increased population. It's *my* intention to continue to part them from enough of their money to tear down the slums of the Five Points, especially the Old Brewery, and build a new, great mission on its site. Do you understand my position?"

I wasn't sure that I did, but I liked her enthusiasm. It was my studied opinion that Eleanor could accomplish anything she set out to do. I regret to say that I had no such confidence in myself. With regard to the Hart case, I felt that I had been blundering about like a bull in a china shop.

# Chapter 39

## GLITTERING GUESTS

The drawing room was softly lit, the flickering light reflected here and there on pastel taffetas, shining brocades, and the jewels of the women. There were perhaps thirty people present.

On the far side of the room was a piano. Poe stood by it, engaged in conversation with a striking woman in black. He told me later that she had been discussing a two thousand dollar cashmere scarf she had bought that afternoon at A.T. Stewart's "on a lark." She was wearing a ring-diamond big enough to support a Five Points family for an indefinite period in comparative luxury. I thought of Mrs. Hart.

"Ah, Sergeant, how are you?" asked Russel McNeil. "I missed speaking with you today at the convention. But I did hear Dr. Whitney's denunciation! If we had more politicians with a tongue quick as hers, I think we'd be better off, don't you?"

Eleanor said: "You give me too much credit. It's simply my nature. I'll leave you two for a moment. But oh," she said, turning back, "first let me introduce you to Mr. and Mrs. John Wendel." She caught the couple's attention and said: "Oh, John, Elizabeth—I'd like you to meet two friends of mine: Detective Sergeant Jonathan Goode, and Russell McNeil of *The Broadway Star.*"

"How do you do, gentlemen," said Mrs. Wendel.

"Mrs. Wendel, you're J.J. Astor's sister, aren't you?"

"That I am, Mr. McNeil. And my brother has told me all about you, I'm afraid," she said, smiling.

McNeil flushed.

"In fact, Mr. McNeil, since that editorial in *The Broadway Star* last month, we've been forbidden to mention your name in my brother's presence." She laughed indulgently.

"Elizabeth," said her husband, "it wasn't as bad as that."

"Well," she explained to McNeil and myself, "ever since that unnameable other newspaper called John a 'self-invented money-making machine' he's not been able to decide whether he was flattered or insulted. It's his uncertainty that makes him angry."

"Sergeant," said John Wendel, attempting to change the subject, "you're not here to watch the jewels, are you?"

"Oh, no, sir," I replied, "it's purely social. Dr. Whitney and I recently met through some common business in the Five Points."

"Eleanor and her social work," said Elizabeth Wendel. "I don't know where you find the time, Eleanor. If Eleanor were more subdued," she said to me, "we could call her an angel of mercy, but as it is . . ."

"I find her efforts most commendable, don't you, Mr. McNeil?" said John Wendel. "I think the ladies are jealous."

"John, you and Elizabeth know," said Eleanor, "that Mr. Whitney left his fortune in my care. I've always felt it my duty to use it for a good purpose. But enough of this unseemly talk. I must take the Sergeant and Mr. McNeil away for a moment. I want them to meet the Schermerhorns."

As soon as we were out of earshot of the Wendels, she said: "Russell, I know you want a moment with Jon alone. I'll leave you and see to the arrangements." Casting a sunshine smile she went west into the clouds of cigar smoke.

"Sergeant," said McNeil, "after the rally I returned to my office and began to write up some of the notes I'd made. Our copy boy told me that I'd had a couple of visitors while I was out. It was Katherine Mary Ross—Red Kate—and the ivory-nosed brute, Mullins. He thoroughly disconcerted the boy. Anyway, Red Kate returned alone, after I'd gotten back. She told me a great deal about Meade's unsavory past. I must say, his moral life leaves much to be desired in a public official. But, of course, that's nothing new."

"I believe I've heard that story, too, McNeil. And I quite agree with you."

"I intend to write an exposé on Meade's origins and his crooked climb in politics. I intend to use every weapon I have to unseat that gangster. We must have him out!"

"I'd like you to know, McNeil, strictly between the two of us, that I may have some interesting material for you shortly. I'm not at liberty to discuss it now, but it does

172

concern direct malfeasance by Meade and I'll confide in you as soon as I have the approval of my superiors. As you know, there is division over Meade in high places, and those who support him are now in the minority."

He glinted his spectacles in a nod. "Fair enough."

"Am I free to believe that you will likewise pass along to me any information you unearth in this matter?"

"Of course."

We turned back to the other guests. I heard Eleanor's voice. "I believe we're all here, now," she said. "Shall we go in to dinner?"

"Jonathan . . ." she said, and gave me her arm.

# Chapter 40

## A SUMPTUOUS REPAST

Two servants opened the great oak sliding doors and we stepped into the dining room.

China, crystal, and silver glittered under a crystal chandelier. On a mahogany sideboard stood two large candelabra, surrounded by silver serving dishes. We passed over a Wilton rug and under portieres of satin. Where it was not hung with valuable pictures and tapestries, dark paneling gleamed.

Eleanor sat at the head of the table. Poe was placed on her right, I on her left. Fleetwood O'Brien sat at the foot, making him Eleanor's rival for table mastery. With Poe at her right, I felt third in importance to her, and a little hurt by it.

"Eleanor," said Poe, as the guests were seating themselves, "how is our little friend, Danny?"

"I think he's been content here with me. At least, he's made no attempt to run away. I think he rather likes me, though I'm constantly correcting and chastising him. I simply adore the little tad. I'm thinking of the possibility of adopting him."

"He's an intelligent boy, isn't he?" I remarked.

"He is," said Eleanor. "As a matter of fact, he's asked me if I could teach him to read. Poor, *poor* little fellow. When I think of the many like him who've been subjected to such unhappy, *miserable* . . ." Her voice trailed off. "He had his dinner about an hour ago and is off to bed now. I'll check in on him later."

The wave of conversation receded as the guests relished their food.

The meal began with a cold, silvery consommé, and cold squab. Then little crabs were served; then hot jellied chicken with asparagus; then pressed duck with chestnut croquettes; then rack of lamb, mint jelly, and an assortment of creamed vegetables. For desert, there was something called meringue a la creme, embedded with fruit. We finished with black coffee. I had never had such belly timber.

"I know the great power Meade has, of course I do," said Fleetwood O'Brien to Wendel, his voice rising, "but we of the Reform Party do not aim to give up. If we don't get rid of him this election, then it'll be the next. It's only a matter of time."

"Jonathan," said Eleanor, "how was Mrs. Hart?"

"She's ready to move," I answered. "We found something among her possessions which may turn out to be a great help to us on this case."

"Oh," she said, "I'm glad to hear it. Have you discovered anything about Mr. Thorndyke's. . . demise? Have you anything to go on, outside of that contemptible note?"

"We may have," I answered.

Poe turned to her: "This is a sumptuous meal. And the claret, I might add, superb." His great, grey, hypnotic eyes stared into hers. I watched him there across the candlelit table and wondered just how he did it. He was speaking of food, and yet his gaze seemed to mean so much more. There's something just too blasted romantic about Eddie, I thought. And immediately I was ashamed of myself.

"Ladies and gentlemen," said Eleanor, getting their attention, "I don't know if you realize it, but Mr. Poe and Sergeant Goode are working together on a murder case, or rather several murders, which involve some of us at the mission. If some of you don't know, the name VanBrunt is involved. I'm sure you all know that name. The accused party is Mr. Peter VanBrunt." The guests murmured.

Someone said, "She means the ne'er do-well VanBrunt, the artist."

"Oh, of course," someone said.

"You might be interested to know," said McNeil, adjusting his spectacles, "that I wrote to the VanBrunt family upon his incarceration, and they responded by saying they had no such relative. *They are all Whigs!*"

"He needs legal counsel," said Eleanor. "Fleetwood," she said, "can't you do something to help the man? I wish you'd go on my behalf and see him. I understand he's being held at the police station on Anthony Street."

"He's been released," I interrupted, "but has suffered an injury. He's at City Hospital, at the moment. Unconscious, in a coma. It may be necessary to operate."

176

"That's my province," said Eleanor, "as a physician. What was the cause of his condition?"

"The attending doctor says he has a concussion."

"Ah, then there's nothing to be done, really. But, Fleetwood, as soon as it's feasible, I want you to see the man. He's entitled to legal counsel. And if his family won't furnish it, I will!"

"You are most gracious," said Poe.

"Mr. Poe," said McNeil, "if you're helping the Sergeant, perhaps you'll tell us something about the difference between solving a real murder and creating one for your fictional detective, C. Auguste Dupin."

"The difference is quite simple. A mystery story is written backwards, its author knowing its solution. Suspense is built because the reader has confidence in the author as to the goal, but is made to share the doubts of the fictional detective. In a real investigation, we begin with a mystery, and must arrive at a solution. But I do think we're on to something. I don't want to speak prematurely, though."

"Oooooh," said the attractive woman in black with the big diamond, "murder . . . it's too horrible. But I must confess, I love mysterious stories."

"I think Mr. Poe underrates himself as a detective," I said. "He's helped me a great deal. His advice has been . . . invaluable." I was a bit conscious-stricken to realize that I'd been piqued by jealousy just a moment before.

177

The table was being cleared.

"Ordinarily, we ladies would leave you gentlemen here to your cigars and brandy," said Eleanor, "but tonight I have something different in mind. We're fortunate to have two distinguished public figures with us. This afternoon we—most of us—heard Mr. O'Brien, whom we believe will soon be the honest Mayor of our great city. And this evening we are fortunate to have one of America's most famous poets with us. If Mr. Poe will consent, we shall hear one of his poems."

Fleetwood O'Brien said: "I think I'm speaking for all present when I ask Mr. Poe to read 'The Raven,' a poem that nearly everyone in the English-speaking world knows."

"Oh, at last," said McNeil, "I can hear it from the author's mouth. 'The Raven,' Poe! Give us 'The Raven'!"

"I shall be honored to do so," said Poe.

The guests fell silent, waiting.

# Chapter 41

## THE RAVEN

"Do you mind, Eleanor?" Poe asked, as he deftly snuffed the flames on the sideboard. He stood by his place at the table with the light of the chandelier dramatically illuminating his face, and began, slowly:

*Once upon a midnight dreary, while I pondered, weak and weary, over many a quaint and curious volume of forgotten lore . . .*

When Eddie recited "The Raven" every syllable was accentuated with such delicacy, and sustained with such sweetness, as I have never heard equaled by other lips. I had read the poem to myself many times, but my ineptitude had given it a sing-song effect. Now I was struck by the grander and more subtle organ tones of the vowels. The guests were still as mannequins, breathless. There seemed no life in the room but Eddie's. I felt under the thrall of a magician until the final words . . .

*And my soul from out that shadow. . . shall be lifted—*nevermore!

For a full minute, Poe and his audience studied each other in silence; then, breaking the mood, he bowed and applause filled the room. The guests crowded around him, complimenting him on his reading, asking about the origins of the poem.

# Chapter 42

## TAKE THIS KISS

I went out on Eleanor's front porch, lit a cigar, and looked over the moonlit expanse of Washington Square.

The square had been a potter's field, and the bones of many a poor soul were beneath it. I fancied the dead looked up with blind sockets, through the sod, to the moon and the stars that were dulled to bronze this night by the black pall of wood smoke that hung over the city. This was the morbid and melancholy state in which Poe's reading had put me.

Bah! I was jealous. Poe was an artist—a poet-performer—doing his work, pushing his fame and fortune, just as I was a policeman, doing my job. I had come to think of him as one with me in my purpose, so helpful had he been. But perhaps that too was part of the alien resentment I felt at the moment. For he was better at my job than I was. His mind worked with speed and efficiency that, in truth, amazed me. He was a genius, and I was merely an ordinary unexceptional man. People put up with his antics, his sometimes arrogance, because of that extraordinary mind, that strange, compelling personality. For once, I felt sunken in my big frame, almost ashamed to be so healthy.

Washington Square by moonlight! I am no poet, but things poetic were leaping about in me. I blew a smoke ring that broke five inches away and blew back into my eyes. I was wiping them, when I thought I saw something out on the field. It looked like a running scarecrow. Poe was giving me dark visions.

Washington Square was now a park, and was sometimes used as a parade field. Somewhere out there in the darkness the old hanging tree still lived, grown old with many rings. In the previous century a young black girl had been hanged from it. She had been charged with taking part in an arson plot. Again, an old scaffold had stood out there for decades. Once, for General Lafayette's benefit, twenty highwaymen were hanged together. It is said that people came by the thousands to enjoy the show.

"What are you doing out here by yourself, Jon?"

"Eleanor . . ."

"It's cold and damp out here. It looks like a night for cold rain."

"But the moon is out. You know, I thought I saw a running scarecrow."

"Eddie has given us all the spooks."

"You shouldn't be out here," I said. "You'll catch cold."

"I have a warm shawl. I wanted to see what you were doing. It was a brilliant reading, wasn't it? Eddie is a genius, but he must suffer so, poor man."

"Poor he is. I have had to finance him."

Dear God, I was ashamed to have blurted that out! I added hastily: "Of course, he'll repay me, I have no doubt."

"Why do you do it?"

"What? Help him out? Oh, it's been well worth it. He's been a tremendous help to me."

"I have no doubt that such a man can be a tremendous help and an equally tremendous hindrance. Sometimes he's not altogether his own man, is he?"

"He's suffering from the loss of his young wife," I said. "He's an honorable fellow."

"And gallant."

"Yes, very."

"Courageous."

"Yes, very."

"You like him, don't you?"

"Yes," I said.

"Kiss me, Jon."

I kissed her.

"It *was* a good reading, wasn't it?" she said.

"Excellent!" I said, suddenly giddy. "Eddie is filled with talent."

It was true. Eddie was an excellent man, and I was proud to say that he was my friend.

# Chapter 43

## THE CRASHER

Inside, I stepped up to Poe, who stood in a circle composed of Fleetwood O'Brien, the beautiful woman in black with the big diamond, the Wendels, McNeil of *The Broadway Star*, a Dr. Sloper, his widowed sister, Mrs. Lavinia Penniman, who was "simply thrilled" at Poe's performance, and his daughter Catherine, a plain, healthy-looking young lady who did not appear to be the heiress of a considerable fortune that she was reputed to be, and several others. The Slopers lived just down Washington Square North from the Whitney house, but were invited as more than close neighbors of Mrs. Whitney, for Dr. Sloper contributed a small amount of his valuable time to improving medical conditions in the Five Points. With the Slopers and yet somehow apart from them was a dandified young man named Morris Townsend. "Sir," he said, "I've read 'The Raven' many times since its publication. I shall never forget my first reading of it—spellbinding—but I should never have fully appreciated the power of its repetitions, especially in the refrain 'Nevermore,' had I not heard you read it. Being without any gifts, your gift strikes me with awe."

"Thank you, sir," said Poe, "but my gift, as you call it, is hard work."

Dr. Sloper made a satisfied snort.

Thus dismissing the obsequious Townsend, Poe turned to me. "Where is Eleanor? What did she think?"

"She thought you were marvelous. She's gone up to look in on the Devlin boy. She's become very attached to him. But what I wanted to say—"

A broken series of screams bounded down the wide stairway, breath-catching, thick-voiced screams, the repeated word "help" attenuated by fear.

There was a jam at the foot of the stairs, where several men collided, myself in the middle. I bulled my way free, took the stairs two at a time, and was first onto the upstairs landing. A long wide hall extended in either direction. Gas lights cast confusing shadows, but toward the end of the hall that led to the front of the house, I spotted a plug-hatted giant, who, as I watched, caught in my own confusion, turned about and dove through the huge stained glass window that overlooked the front of the house and Washington Square beyond. A chaos of glittering, colored shards of sharp glass followed him out. Later that night, one of the cabmen who waited in front of the house said that the figure bursting through the window with splinters of glass in a multi-colored aura about him looked like "the prince of darkness himself in flight." Our man did not fly, however, but fell, and landed with such crushing weight on the stone steps of the house that his spiked shoes chipped out chunks of brownstone from the smooth surface. The cabman said that he hit with a deep knee bend, but immediately rose, in huge proportions, and took the ten steps up in one leap down, hitting the sidewalk running.

Ahead of me and to the side, I could hear weeping. It was Danny Devlin. Then I heard Eleanor consoling him. I found the door and stepped in. Eleanor ran into my arms. "Oh, thank God, Jon!" she cried. "I opened the door. It was dark. I didn't bring a lamp because we have the hall lighting. I came over to the bed to find a lamp. Then I saw silhouetted in the moonlight from the window a giant with a top hat *smothering* Danny with a pillow! Before I could scream, he hit me across the chin with something. I don't remember anything else."

"Could you identify him?"

"No. Just that he was huge, and that top hat . . ."

Danny said: "He was wearing a scarf tied over his face! When he let the pillow go, I started yelling me head off. He ran out the door."

For a tender moment the three of us stood and held each other like a little family. Then I said, "You're safe now. I must try to catch him." I let them go and stepped into the hall.

"Poe!" I exclaimed. He was kicking the glass from the window sill. In an instant he had climbed out the window. He hung there another instant, dropped, crossed the street, and disappeared into Washington Square Park.

At the window, I was hit by a fine, cold rain. The sky lightened with a jagged strike, and I spotted the giant, who now took on the aspect of a running scarecrow. He was off, among the trees, his long scarf flying behind him, toward Washington Square South, probably trying to make it to

Thompson Street. I went back down through a house full of alarmed guests and out into the street, where the carriage horses were pushing the carriages backward and jerking them forward, and giving their drivers great difficulty in controlling them. A few of the horses and a few of the men were bleeding from the flying glass. I entered the park at a nearby gate and was immediately flung headlong over something soft and moaning.

"Poe?" I questioned, getting up.

"It's me, Wilson. Go on, Sarge, I'm all right. He just sapped me."

There was a shot. I ran deeper into the park. There was another shot. The sky lightened, and I saw Poe about fifty yards ahead of me, to the east. The rain was coming harder now, wind-blown in waves. There was another shot. Three shots, then a fourth.

"The beggar's got a pepperbox," I told the rain. "He's got two left."

I saw the fifth, like a firefly, flare a hundred yards ahead. I lunged into Poe. "Hang back, Jon, he said. "He must have one left. It's no good at anything beyond twenty yards, but I don't know where he is."

"He's way off ahead there," I said. "I saw the last shot."

"Then we've lost him," said Poe.

In the face of the dark, and the now needling rain, I had to concede the point.

## Chapter 44

## LEFTOVERS

About faced, Washington Square North, with its lighted windows, presented a picture of plutocratic safety. I was now struck by the enormity of what had occurred. The rich of the Fifteenth Ward, who were, in their daily rounds, scarcely aware of the existence of the denizens of the Sixth Ward, which is to say the Five Points and environs, had actually been invaded by an archetype of the Sixth. The indifferently smug social order had been breeched. The Frog and Toe had visited the Progressive City.

"How's Eleanor?" Poe asked, as we trudged back to the house.

"She caught a glancing blow from a blackjack. But no serious damage."

"And the boy?"

"Tough little mugger. Nothing wrong with him."

"What actually happened? How did he get in? Do you know?"

"The Oulde Sixth Ward has finally had the temerity to attack the Fifteenth," I told him, echoing my own thoughts. "There was a policeman's leather helmet by the bed, and a huge cape in the hall. Since he was wearing his plug hat, it would seem he carried it in under his cape. When he got close to the house he changed and walked in like a working copper, I presume."

"Strange," said Poe, "when Eleanor entered the room she must have been in full view, the hall light behind her. Unmistakable, I should think."

"What are you getting at?"

"The rogue had a repeating pistol, a pepperbox. Why didn't he shoot her? That was the gist of the threat on the note— Dr. Whitney beware!"

"Didn't want us coming up . A shot would have brought us."

"No faster than a scream, and he had to let the boy loose in order to hit Eleanor. And consider, why was he after the boy? What do the Plug Uglies have to do with the Devlin boy? He can only help to show that VanBrunt did not kill Mary Hart. But the fact is, the Plug-Ugly was trying to kill the boy. Another fact is, that he did not try to kill Eleanor."

"It is odd, isn't it?"

"And out here in the dark, and a considerable distance ahead, he'd have been better off not shooting and showing his location," Poe ruminated. "Then why did he do it?"

"To kill you?"

"That's an unpleasant thought, Jon."

I ventured, "It could have been Mullins."

189

Poe said, "It could have been Boss Meade himself, or—how many Plug-Uglies are there, Jon? The gang is famous for giantism, and they deliberately add to the illusion of their great height by wearing those plug hats. It could have been any of them—perhaps a lonely emissary sent by Meade himself."

I had to concede the point.

Wilson waited at the open door, holding a palm to the back of his head. Shards of stained glass lay everywhere underfoot. I hated to think of the replacement cost of that huge stained-glass window. It had portrayed one of the late Mr. Whitney's sources of wealth, a full-rigged cargo ship. Eleanor had apparently directed that a quilt be hung at the empty window frame. It portrayed a much humbler vision of flowers. They were being watered by the miniature squall now underway. Wilson said, "I'm sorry, Sarge. It was all so sudden."

"Are you all right?"

He nodded. "You gotta mean business if you wanna kill a man with a sap."

"Did somebody mean business when he hit VanBrunt," asked Poe, "or was it just an abundance of malice that overcame better judgment?"

"You think it was the same person?"

"There are plenty of blackjacks around," Poe said, "and too many cleavers."

190

# Chapter 45

## RAIN ON THE PARADE

Eleanor was incensed. "Even in my own house—and with a policeman outside, a police sergeant and a candidate for mayor inside. Meade knows no limits."

The guests milled about in the hallway, some fetching their hats and coats, all in great anxiety. Eleanor said hurried good-nights as they filed out.

Poe took me aside. "I've got an idea," he said. "But let's wait until everyone's gone."

I advised the stragglers to depart, and in a few moments only Eleanor, the servants, Danny, McNeil, and Fleetwood O'Brien remained.

"May I suggest," said Poe, "that Danny be moved for safe-keeping. In fact, I think he might be best off out of the city."

"Out of the city?" Eleanor did not like the idea.

"I have a home—a cottage, merely—at Fordham," Poe said. "We could take him by carriage, Mr. Wilson riding lookout to see that we are not followed. It's now clear that, as I had feared, this boy's life is in danger. If the Plug Uglies are behind this, I wouldn't put it past them to storm the house, and neither would I put it beyond them to discover where we had the boy hidden, if he remained in the city."

"That's right," I said, "we know they had a spy at *The Broadway Star*."

"If there are spies in *The Broadway Star*," cried McNeil, outraged, "I shall discover them—and have them out!"

"There must be spies in the ranks of the police, as well," said Poe. "No, the boy must be gotten out of this city. Our enemies have reached a point of arrogance hitherto unknown."

"If so," said Eleanor, "I'm going with him. And we shall use my carriage."

"We'll all go," I said. I called Wilson and asked him if he could handle a team. He said that he could, and I told him to prepare Eleanor's carriage for a long ride.

"It'll be Eddie, Eleanor, Danny, myself, with Wilson driving."

"Must we travel by night?" asked Eleanor.

"It's better so," said Poe. "If we're followed, we can lose our pursuers. There's no way to tell what can happen next here in the city—or, indeed, in this house."

# Chapter 46

## ESCAPE

Hail tapped with skeleton digits on the carriage top. Wind whistled between gapped, icy teeth. I stuck my head out into the cruel weather to see and dismiss many plug-hatted pursuers, giant white figures striped with shadows, running even alongside the carriage on enormously long legs, their eyes burning in the night like red coals with hatred.

Finally cobblestones gave out, and we were on a raw, rutted country road, our wheels turning up mud that flew like trout climbing falls, and closed on our flanks by dark legions of sometimes swaying, sometimes whipping trees. The glow of the city receded behind us, the black vacuum of the woods engulfed us, and all we had for light were the short, shaking casts of our carriage lamps.

"No fear of highwaymen tonight," I said, trying to comfort Eleanor. "Bandits do not need to work in rough weather, as do honest men, like poor Wilson, atop, and cold and drenched by now, I should think. I wouldn't want to be a coachman, though withal, I don't suppose it's much different from being a sailor, exposed to weather, as I have been." I seemed to sound a heartier note than I felt. I didn't know the degree of Henchard's corruption, and it had occurred to me that he might have set the police against me, against all of us who were attempting to escape the Frog and Toe. It was difficult to assess how much trouble we were in, and it is at such times that the imagination steps in with its gift of exaggeration. There were moments when I felt that we in the carriage were the last of a hunted breed.

Danny Devlin had burrowed into Eleanor's side, under her protective arm, as well as several blankets, and had fallen asleep. My lady Eleanor's head bent over him, as if to kiss the tyke. Strength of mind and gentleness of heart combined in her to bring forth the highest regard of others—she was the very portrait of a lady. Look, as we bounced most miserably, only she did not groan and grimace, as Poe and I did, but looked up occasionally with a half smile of contentment, while her blue eyes shown with an eagerness for the rough and dangerous adventure. Even the slight bruise on her chin, where she had been hit, lent to her firm but feminine features the dash of pugnacity, of daring. A rich woman, or any woman, but even more so a woman who might have lived an easy and uncomplicated life, it must have taken much courage for such a woman to have apprenticed herself to medicine in our age of brutes, uneducated and educated alike. My admiration knew no bounds.

"Does Wilson know the way to Fordham?" I asked Poe.

"I gave him instructions," he said. "I usually commute by boat, or by the Harlem Railroad, so I am no expert at the roads, but I think Wilson will get us safely there within three more hours, despite the weather, and then, my friends, you will meet my mother-in-law, Mrs. Clemm, who is dearer to me than anyone now on this earth, and our cat, Caterina, who has a soul. I call my mother-in-law 'Muddy,' for that was what my Virginia called her before she could pronounce the word mother. Muddy is all that I have left of Virginia now—or of anything."

194

Poe took a long draft from a bottle of rum. He seemed distant, ruminative.

"You shouldn't drink so much, Eddie," said Eleanor, "for your health's sake alone, which is enough, but also because we are all depending on you to help us get out of our difficulties."

"Of course you are right," said Poe. "I'm sorry, I quite forgot myself. But would anyone else like a drink, to warm themselves?"

"One to warm up on," I said, and took a draft from the bottle.

"Three hours to the Domain of Arnheim," said Poe. "It can be done in half the time by boat, up the Hudson, by the palisades, through the narrows to where the gorge opens on all beauty."

"Are you quite all right, Eddie?" asked Eleanor, with a note of alarm, for he looked very strange and excited.

"I am agitated at the thought of meeting Annie once again."

"Who is Annie?" I asked.

"Annie! Annabelle Lee! *Helen*—"

"Eddie! Eddie!" Eleanor reached out and touched his forehead. "He's burning with fever."

There was a long snarl from the sky and for an instant daylight abounded inside the carriage. In the flash I had seen

195

Poe's face. The grey of his great eyes seemed to have turned black in the white-ringed, dark-circled sockets.

"In spring, the turf is green and delicious. Virginia and I go for walks, like children, in bare feet. There are jasmine, and sweet honeysuckle, and a grape vine, and a dead pear tree clothed from head to foot in gorgeous begonia blossoms—locusts, catalpas, elm, oak, and tulip trees, a sort of magnolia—all under and over and around us—Virginia and I. That is Arnheim where Landor's cottage can be found."

Great trees along the roadside bowed over us, rustling with ice now. As the miles passed, Poe fell into a fitful sleep. He groaned and shifted about. Eleanor took his pulse. She said:

"His pulse beats only ten regular beats, then it suspends or becomes intermittent. I don't think it can be simply the fever."

"What do you mean?"

"He may have a heart condition."

"My God! I didn't know."

"I can't be sure, Jon. It's just—"

"What can we do?"

"For the present—nothing. Just get him to bed as soon as possible."

"Snowing!" called down Wilson, faint in the wind.

Yes, the tapping of rain, sleet, and hail had stopped. There was a soft swirling of the air now.

"It's early for snow," I said, troubled all around. "We could find ourselves snowbound without adequate provisions."

Poe lurched forward, wide-eyed.

"Jon," he cried excitedly, "where's your razor?"

"What do you want a razor for, Eddie?"

"To shave off my mustache."

"What do you want to do that for, Eddie?" I asked, pushing him back in his seat and covering him with a blanket.

"So that they won't recognize me."

"Who?"

"The killers who are after me."

I looked at Eleanor.

"He's hallucinating," she said.

"This happened earlier today, but I thought he was over it. I don't know," I said, "if this whole trip isn't a mistake. Eddie presented the idea to me so quickly, right after the attack on Danny and you, and with such assurance, that I fell in with it. He has a way of taking charge of things. Something of the Sergeant-Major remains with him. But I wonder now if it wasn't just the homing instinct of a sick man."

"No," said Eleanor, "Eddie's right. If a gangster can invade a home on Washington Square, anything can happen. The only safe place for Danny is out of the city, and why not at Eddie's?"

"But why did you come along, Eleanor? There was no need. I could have driven Poe and the boy up here, and Wilson could have stayed in town and watched over your safety."

"I didn't want to be separated from Danny so soon. I wanted to see him into safety. Look at him, sound asleep. I have good reason to fear Meade myself. Nor did I want to be separated from you, Jon." She reached out and took my hand. Thus the dark miles passed.

# Chapter 47

## HOME IS THE HUNTER

At two in the morning we arrived at the cottage. As we reined in, I could see little in the checkered light but a low white slope of roof. A door opened, golden in the darkness, casting a carpet of light toward the carriage. A large, lamp-bearing woman tossed more light about as she made her way unsteadily down a cloudlike carpet of snow toward us.

Poe emerged from the carriage like a drunken man.

"Oh! Eddie! Eddie!" cried Mrs. Clemm. "Eddie, come here, my dear boy! Let me put you to bed!"

"He isn't drunk," I said. "He's sick."

"He has a fever," said Eleanor. I'm Dr. Whitney, Eddie's friend. I'm a physician. I'm going to take care of him."

"What'll I do with the horses, Sarge?" Wilson asked.

"There's a shed off toward the hill," said Mrs. Clemm, pointing to the back of the cottage. We appeared to be in a very isolated spot. Values of both safety and danger ran through my mind. Supporting Poe, we crunched our way through the new-fallen snow and into the cottage.

"Where are we?" asked Poe.

"Why, you're home, Eddie," said Mrs. Clemm, "home with Muddy. I've been worried about you."

"Don't worry, Muddy, everything's going to be all right."

"Of course it is, Eddie. Of course it is."

She led us to a settee beside a cold dead fireplace. Indeed, the cottage was very cold. "Put him here," she said. "I'll start a fire. Eddie filled the shed with wood before he left. I've been saving it for when he came home."

"Where is the wood?" I asked.

"Through the kitchen, down the steps—the woodshed's attached to the cottage."

"Good, we'll soon have a fire in every room," I said, turning to fetch the wood.

When I returned, Eleanor said: "Jon, help us get Eddie out of his wet clothes."

"But these aren't his clothes," said Mrs. Clemm.

"They are borrowed, ma'am," I said.

Doctor and mother-in-law and I stripped our charge and redressed him, at my insistence, in street clothes. I wanted Eddie prepared in case of an invasion. I was surprised to see in what apparently good condition he was, trim, and quite muscular, unlike one who does sedentary work. I commented on this.

"Oh, he exercises. He does chin-ups on the trees and goes off running through the woods. He goes occasionally to a gymnasium in the city," said Mrs. Clemm. "He has always taken pride in his physique."

"He may have overtaxed himself," said Eleanor. "Does he ever complain of shortness of breath or of chest pains?"

"He's not a complainer, though the world has treated him most unfairly."

"Does he eat well?"

Mrs. Clemm shook her head. "We don't often have much," she said. "He'll eat a pretzel and coffee, and maybe a bit of fruit, or buttermilk and curds, for breakfast. We often only have dandelion greens for supper. I gather them from the fields and boil them. But now that winter's here . . . ." She shook her head. "His friends are always willing to give Eddie a drink, but not a meal."

"What is that scar he has across his shoulder?" I asked. "It looks to have been a serious wound."

"He will only say that it is connected to an affair of honor and that it happened while he was in the military. He served three years in the army, you know," she added proudly, "and rose to the rank of Sergeant-Major."

"Yes, I did know," I said.

Mrs. Clemm showed me about the cottage. It was simply furnished. There was an ingrain carpet on the floor of the main room. At the windows were white muslin curtains. In

201

the two small upstairs rooms there were merely beds and a chair and table. The main room boasted a rocking-chair, the settee upon which Poe was now sleeping, two hanging bookcases, and a writing desk.

I set the fires going, and we reconvened in the kitchen, where Wilson stood, shaking the snow from himself. We sat down over hot coffee.

# Chapter 48

## EUREKA

Mrs. Clemm was a large woman, almost mannish in aspect. Her widow's cap gave her the look of one in mourning, which indeed she was, for her daughter had died less than a year ago, in January, or the appearance of some kind of secular nun. There was a stoicism about her, but no trace of martyrdom.

We explained to her in some detail who we were and how we came to be there. When she understood, she said: "Of course. I'm sure Eddie knows best. Whatever he's planned, it will be perfectly satisfactory to me. You're all quite welcome."

"I've been worried about Eddie's health for days," I said. "I've tried to get him to eat, take better care of himself—"

"Oh, I know how ill he is, sir," she said. "He's often like this now, since Virginia's death. He's my nephew, you understand, as well as my son-in-law. He and Virginia were first cousins. The Poes are a high-strung family. They came out of County Cowan, Ireland, and have certain of the Celtic tendencies—as well as the Celtic gifts. But I love Eddie as if he were my own son. It galls me that, despite his fame, we remain so poor. And it's not that he doesn't work. He works like a Trojan, but, somehow . . ." She brightened. "Even now he's composing his greatest work."

"What is the subject, if I may ask?"

"It's the solution to the riddle of the universe. He calls it *Eureka*. Eddie cannot stand to be alone, so, when he writes, I sit nearby, and sew or do some small domestic chore, and occasionally he rises and asks me to walk about with him outside. He needs the air to refresh him. Then he tells me what he's writing. I don't understand much of it, so he asks me what it is that I don't understand, and I tell him, and he explains it again, and sometimes I can understand it, then. The universe, everything, he says, was only one particle in space that exploded, and became all that we know. He has a way of explaining it. He often reads and recites to me and I enjoy it more than anything in the world. But listen to me going on when you must be exhausted. Look at this boy— did you say his name's Danny?—he's asleep in his chair. Shouldn't we get him to bed?"

"Jeese!" cried Danny, his eyes popping open, "I don't wanna go to bed. I'm not sleepy. I slept in the carriage. I'm wide awake."

"And in five minutes," said Eleanor, "you're going to be narrow asleep, or my name isn't Eleanor Vance Whitney."

# Chapter 49

## NIGHTWATCH

That night, Eleanor and Mrs. Clemm shared one of the upstairs rooms; Danny was put to bed in the other. Wilson and I were to take turns in the small downstairs room, the one, I was to learn, in which Virginia had died, wrapped in Poe's old army coat, and with Caterina upon her chest for warmth. Wilson and I felt that one of us should stand watch in case we had been followed. I took the first watch, sitting at the kitchen table, with a cigar, coffee, and a book of Poe's poems, and Caterina in my lap for company.

I sat for nearly an hour, reading, listening to the wind shivering the trees, and thinking over the day's events. I got up to poke the fire and had my back to the room, when I was startled by a sound behind me. I turned to see Poe edging his way down on a chair at the table. He gave me a hard look, and said, with sudden delight:

"Ah, VanBrunt! I'm glad you're here. I knew you'd take me up on my invitation. Spring is the most beautiful time to visit us here in the country. You're going to stay for a week. Virginia and Muddy will be delighted. Tomorrow we'll go hiking. Look out the window," he cried, with a sudden burst of energy, pointing, "the cherry trees are in blossom. Their petals are falling like snow. You and Virginia and I will walk over to St. John's University. I have a dear friend there—a priest and professor. You can always count on good conversation. In fact, he even seems to understand

*Eureka*—though of course he disagrees. But I tell him there is nothing to disagree about; it is merely a different way of saying the same thing. 'Let there be light,' and there was one particle of light, and that light blossomed into everything." He thumped the table with a fist. "I don't know why everyone should find it complicated, do you?"

"Eddie," I said. I put my hands on his shoulders, looked into his troubled, confused eyes. "Eddie, it's me, Jonathan. VanBrunt isn't here!"

He returned my gaze, questioningly, and suddenly slumped down in his seat, put his arms on the table, and dropped his head onto them, as though completely exhausted, spent.

"I don't know how Muddy puts up with me sometimes," he said in a muffled voice to the tabletop. With great effort, he raised his head, took my arms, drew me close, and whispered, conspiratorially: "Blow my brains out, Jon. Put an end to it, this fever called living."

"Eddie," I said, putting an arm over his shoulders, "come, lie down. You're sick and overwrought."

I helped him back to the settee, where he stretched out, and covered him with a blanket.

I had intended to deliver Danny into safe hands and to return to the city as soon as possible. I had not foreseen Poe's illness, though perhaps I should have, had my mind not been preoccupied with the case. But Poe had fallen ill in my service, as it were, and I felt it my duty to see him through.

Just before dawn, I put down *Tamerlane and Other Poems*, and rubbed my tired eyes. A dismal light shown at the windows. I got up from the table, stretching, and looked out. The long night was nearly over.

## Chapter 50

## WHO GOES THERE?

Because of the angle, I could not see much to the west. In the east a few stars paled in the lightening sky.

A few yards from the house, beneath the trees, something moved in the thick, shadowy underbrush. I strained to see what it was. Had my tired eyes been playing a trick? No, the underbrush was being disturbed, bending and tossing. Perhaps it was a deer . . . perhaps a bear . . . or perhaps an Indian. Then came a darker thought, in the form of a question. Had we been followed, after all?

My hair stood on end as I heard a scream of agony. Grabbing my pistol from the table, I fairly threw my bulk from the kitchen into the main room from where the scream had seemed to come. But now I saw that it was Poe who had cried out, from the depths of a nightmare. He was still muttering, tossing about. I did what I could to calm him, shaking him, speaking words of reassurance. When he was quiet, I hurried back to the kitchen, and peered out the window. All was still.

I wondered if I should wake Wilson and tell him what had happened. But what *had* happened? I'm not given to nervousness, but I felt decidedly edgy. The sensation embarrassed me. I decided to keep my fears to myself until something definite happened. I took up my post at the window, nervously thumbing back the hammer of my pistol and releasing it, cocking and uncocking the weapon. I became aware of what I was doing and placed the pistol on the window sill. Now I checked my watch—just past five in the morning. I stared into the surrounding woods, trying to see into, around, beyond, *through* the shadow-clad trees. I don't know how long I stood thus, transfixed, how often I left the window to go to the stove for coffee; but at last, as the morning brightened, and I could look into the clear image of nature, I found myself holding an empty cup. I went to fill it and returned to the window, sipping the stale, steaming brew, to discover a musket-bearing man dismounting in the clearing beyond the woodshed.

I dropped my cup, spilling the hot liquid down my thigh, and grabbed up my pistol and cocked it. But then I saw the unconcern of the man. There was nothing stealthy about his approach, nothing threatening. Indeed, his plain, open face looked as if it were preparing a greeting for the morning. As my eyes dropped to the musket at his side, they passed a glinting something. I looked back to see a star. He was a policeman of some sort.

I opened the door.

"Good morning," I called.

"Morning. I'm Crenshaw, constable of Fordham Village. Thought I'd get out early this morning and check on the neighbors. See everything's all right. Some times there are accidents, you know, especially when folks aren't prepared for such an early storm."

"Thank you, Constable. We're all fine," I said. "I'm Sergeant Goode of the Municipal Police, New York City, here on business." I showed him my star. "Tell me, did you see anyone about while you were making your rounds?"

"Around here?"

"Yes. Any strangers?"

"No. Only yourself. Why?"

"I thought I saw someone out there in the trees awhile ago."

"*I* was by here about an hour ago, on my way out to the Valentine mansion. Perhaps you saw me."

"About an hour ago? It must have been you. It's a relief. I thought we were being stalked by an Indian."

"Only a few friendly Indians around here. I saw the light when I passed earlier and thought I'd stop on my way back to the village and make sure Mrs. Clemm was all right. I know Mr. Poe keeps odd hours. Sometimes the lights are on all night. But I'd heard he was in the city, and thought maybe she was alone and might be sick or something."

"She's fine," I said, "but Mr. Poe is ill."

"Oh, sorry to hear that. Is it serious?"

"Nothing fatal, I think. There's a doctor here and he's in good care. Would you like to come in for a cup of very bad coffee, Constable?"

"Well, sir, there's nothing I'd like better. But perhaps another time. If everything's under control, I should be getting back to the village. Much to do there, after such weather. Need every Jack Cove they can get." He mounted his horse. "Nice to meet you. Look for me in the village if you need anything. Let me know how Mr. Poe's getting on."

He spurred his horse away. Before he entered the woods, he turned, gave the cottage a last look, and saluted me with a wave of his hand.

I felt reassured by his proximity. But for the time being there was no need to tell him any more of our business. That he did not ask more than he needed to know, gave me a good opinion of Crenshaw. The Constable was a man of judgment and discretion.

# Chapter 51

## A DREAM WITHIN A DREAM

On the third day, Poe's fever broke, and I encouraged Eleanor to get out of the cottage, for her own health's sake—for she had attended him at all hours and with the greatest care—as, indeed, she had us all. Leaving Wilson on watch, and Muddy in charge of medical and domestic matters, Eleanor and I set St. John's University as the goal of our outing.

All traces of snow had vanished. The wet leaves clung to our feet as we walked beneath the near-naked trees, exchanging early experiences and our desires and aims for the future. Although I found my affection for Eleanor to be increasing with the minutes, I felt that a certain reserve was proper in the circumstances. I did not wish to take advantage of the enforced intimacy of the situation. As we crossed a purling little brook, she took my hand, quite naturally, and, when we were secure on the opposite bank, did not release it. Compelled against reserve, I did not release hers. What followed, as she stepped ahead of me, holding my hand, and blocking my path, was like a wondrous, slow, and precise dance. I found her in my arms, her lips pressed with startling passion against mine. I was breathless with surprise. The isolation, the craggy landscape, the coagulating, flying clouds against the dark blue afternoon sky, the sun against it in strands, like gold beaten to airy thinness, the startled flapping, the wild dark break-away through the trees of a flock of crows—these were part of the moment. I pushed her from me and held her at arm's length. Her mouth was open, loose, her eyes half shut. I drew her back to my chest, half-consciously, effortlessly.

Afterwards, we went on. I said nothing for a time, because I desired to say the right thing when I spoke. I was in love, but deeply troubled. It was she who broke the silence.

"Jonathan, I love you."

"Can you mean that, Eleanor?"

"I try to say what I mean, Jon."

After a time, I was able to overcome my embarrassment, and broached the subject that troubled me.

"We are too far apart," I said. "I was struck dumb by love when I met you. Poe had to speak for me, remember? But that was love at first sight—in other words, powerful attraction. Now that I know you, I can't imagine a life without you. Now that you return my love—something that I couldn't have imagined—now that the situation is real, is serious, even possible, it takes on new and different meaning. I'm a bit of a snob, I fear. I'm just a poor policeman. You're rich."

"I'm rich, I guess, but through my husband, as you well know. What you don't know is that Eleanor Vance was a nurse, hired by an aging man who married her and sent her through medical training because that was the price she put upon the marriage. Nevertheless, I come from the same stock as yourself, good honest Yankee merchants." She laughed, mockingly. "Oh, Jon! Shall I give Mr. Whitney's money away? Then will you have me?"

"I must make my own fortune." Oh, but I sounded pompous!

"What! As a policeman? It would take ten lifetimes. My husband was very rich. Better simply do as I do, and try to ignore my wealth. Then I shall marry you and adopt little Danny. We'll scandalize New York society. What do you say?"

She laughed gently, then hummed a little tune the rest of the way.

## Chapter 52

## MY FAULT

That evening, as I sat beside Danny, who was listening to one of Muddy's stories, I put an arm over his shoulders in camaraderie. He looked up at me and blurted, "Jeese, I wish you wus me dad," and, breaking loose, ran from the room. I looked for relief to Eleanor, who looked back enigmatically, in such a way as to give no relief, no hint of compassion, and I felt that, somehow, in some way that eluded me, everything wrong with the world was my fault.

# Chapter 53

## BREAKING CAMP

Once his fever had broken, Poe improved rapidly. Eleanor remarked on his resilience. "I must have been wrong about his heart," she told me. "He is essentially healthy. I have never seen anyone come back so quickly from such a fever. His constitution is good. His problems stem from the way he lives. But it's very difficult to tell a genius what to do."

One evening, as Eleanor and I played chess, Poe sat up and offered suggestions about our game, being charmingly annoying. Then, enlarging on the subject, he insisted that whist was a much more difficult game than chess, and that it required more intelligence, as chess, in his opinion, required more intelligence than did mathematics. The latter he described as "a simple logical progression without the complicating factor of human nature."

Poe's poverty outraged Eleanor. "That a man of his fame, talent, and industry should be so reduced is a disgrace—not to him, but to us. Mrs. Clemm has no money at all. She's sometimes compelled to take a basket to her neighbors and actually beg for food. A woman of her dignity! She's very brave. Do you know," she went on, "that they pay only a hundred dollars a year for the cottage? A man named Valentine owns it. And yet it's difficult for them. But look at his work! He's constantly in print. Does no one pay him properly? Scoundrels! They pirate his work."

Now that Poe was on the mend, I thought it time for Wilson and I to get back to the city. "We've got to get back on the case. I'm going to be handicapped without Poe, but I can't stay here any longer."

I was certain now that we had not been followed. I felt that Muddy, Poe, and Danny would be safe enough. Then, too, there was Constable Crenshaw's ever-watchful eye. I'd spoken with him several times since the first morning and knew him to be dependable. But Eleanor decided that she would stay at Fordham, help Mrs. Clemm with Poe and Danny, and give her some support in general. "I'll stay for a week perhaps, or until you're able to settle things with Meade, and come back."

"Then we'll leave you the carriage," I said. "We can hire someone in the village to take us to the train. But how will you get back if you should want to leave sooner—I mean, before I can get back, or have someone come up to drive the carriage for you?"

"I can hire a man in the village to drive me back, if necessary, but it won't be. And I'll have you know that I can handle the carriage myself, if I have to."

"Well," I said, "I know that Muddy will be pleased at your staying. She'll need all the help she can get. You have a good heart, my dear."

"So do you, my Jon—that's why I love you."

"Only that?"

"I won't make you vain, Jon. But I'll keep you proud."

217

# Chapter 54

## THE WARRANT

On Thursday, the 23rd, Poe, Wilson and I returned to New York on the Harlem Railroad. We had been out of town for the best part of five days, during which Poe had recovered; nevertheless, it was against Eleanor's advice that he returned to the case. But he was intractable. "I must finish what I undertake to do," he told Eleanor. "It is a matter of conscience with me." If truth be told, he did not look too badly, the enforced rest having afforded his recuperative powers the opportunity they needed.

Poe left me at Police Headquarters at City Hall, and went to fetch Mrs. Hart's Bible. I had discovered in him a man of duty, punctilious even in small matters, and honor-bound where his word was concerned. Ten minutes later I was back on the street, in company with Wilson and two burly leatherheads. I saw Poe approaching at a quick pace, wearing a long black cape.

"Was it ready?" I asked him.

In answer he lifted away the left side of the cape, displaying a large, heart-level inside pocket, and the top of the re-bound Bible. "The cape is a loan from the bookbinder," he said. "He's an old friend. He did a fine job on the Bible. Too bad Mrs. Hart can't see it, but her hands, at least, will be able to approve it."

I handed him the warrant.

"What's this?"

"Read it."

"Too much glare," he said, handing it back. "Tell me."

"It's a warrant for the arrest of Boss Meade on several counts of malfeasance, including bribery, extortion, misappropriation of city funds, etc. My superiors have been able to substantiate several of the allegations made in Lucy Brody's diary. In fact, they've been holding the warrant for a couple of days for me to serve, as a reward for my work on the case. You've made a name for me in the department, Eddie."

"I'm sure Meade has enemies who have been waiting to leap upon him," said Poe.

"Yes," I said. "They've made me an acting captain. Apparently they don't want me outranked by Captain Henchard, who is also under suspicion. Indeed, I've been ordered to arrest him, if he interferes. It's been suggested that the Mayor's against Meade, because Meade has usurped some of the graft floating around, and has put pressure on Chief Matsell to act against him. These are very serious charges. Meade might cut and run. But, if he doesn't, he might blow Matsell out of office in revenge. Meade's attempts to get me off the case have backfired. I think we have him."

"But not for murder."

"That will come."

"Perhaps."

I lit a cigar. It annoyed me that Eddie did not seem to share in my enthusiasm. But then, Eddie could be a very irritating, as well as charming, fellow. When you were looking here, he was looking there. He kept one off balance.

"All right, men," I said to the others, "let's go."

# Chapter 55

## DANGEROUS FACTIONS AT ODDS

As we turned into Anthony Street I noticed an unusual number of Sixth Ward patrolmen with their copper stars pinned to their chests and surly expressions on their faces. A crowd of them had gathered in front of the Anthony Street Station. As we walked by, one of them said to me, "Don't try it." It was clear that Meade knew we were coming, had been tipped off.

"This has the shapings of a riot—a police riot," I said to Poe.

One of the Headquarters cops said, "We should have brought pistols."

We continued down the street. I said to Poe: "Meade cannot plan to resist arrest. What good would it do? Headquarters would only send reinforcements—and the army, if necessary."

Poe said: "If he does resist, he will have another purpose in mind."

"Pray tell, what would that be?"

"To create havoc, during which to make his escape. One of us should watch the American Saloon closely, to see to it that he doesn't escape, while another man goes back to Headquarters for reinforcements adequate to the situation."

"It's too late. I cannot alter the situation now," I said. "I'm under orders. But why do you suppose he hasn't fled already?"

"Clearly," said Poe, "he's just been notified of his impending arrest by some Headquarters spy who has run ahead of us. He probably wants time to gather what stolen loot he can to take with him."

As we approached the American Saloon I said to Wilson: "I want you to come with Poe and me. We'll go through the saloon. You other two go into the alley and come in the back. Meade's office is right by the back door.

"Now listen, you two Headquarters boys—and Wilson, too—some of these Sixth Ward policemen may try to stop us. Badge or no badge, treat any officer who gets in your way as an outlaw."

# Chapter 56

## NOT WELCOME

We stepped into the American Saloon. It was a veritable museum of patriotism. Amid the red, white, and blue of the place were hung old campaign posters. The heroes of Tammany looked solemnly down on us from a portrait gallery as we made our way breathlessly to the rear, amid Plug Uglies and Sixth Ward leatherheads. The bar ran the length of the left side of the room. On the right, scattered tables. The policemen leaned against the bar displaying their stars, some menacingly twirling their billy clubs. The Plug Uglies sprawled at the tables, some displaying the spikes of their brogans on table tops. A few Plug Uglies slapped the flats of their cleavers on the palms of their hands, or patted them where they dangled from leather thongs from their belts. As we passed a Sixth Ward copper with whom I'd been friendly, he whispered under his breath, "Better back off!"

A glint of brass knuckles caught my eye. Every policeman in the saloon owed his job to Boss Meade, and they were there to protect their interest. Faces I knew, faces full of rancor and jealousy, angry eyes everywhere.

A Plug Ugly stood in front of Meade's office door, his arms folded across his chest. I told him to stand aside. He merely smiled, hideously displaying teeth that had been filed to vicious points. He was a foot taller than I, but weighed no more. I heaved my bulk into him, pushing him aside, and pulled open the door.

Meade and Captain Henchard stood behind a big desk, flanked by two policemen wearing badges. Seated at a table were Legs and Butt, the two butchers who had fixed Boodle Coign's wagon.

Poe, Wilson, and I were outnumbered several to one. I hoped that the two Headquarters boys would enter by the back door, evening the odds.

"Alderman Meade, I've come to execute this warrant for your arrest. It comes from Chief Matsell and the Mayor of the City of New York, under the auspices of the Governor of the State of New York. I must advise you that it is your duty as a citizen to quietly submit to arrest."

"I will not submit!" Meade shouted. "Give me that, you turncoat traitor!" He snatched the warrant and tore it to pieces.

"I shall have to take you by force," I said.

Legs and Butt began to laugh, then the two policemen joined in. Then Captain Henchard. At last Meade broke into soft, menacing smile. Suddenly he frowned. I was looking now, not at the politician, but at the Plug Ugly of years before, a gray old cruel giant, made even more dangerous by the cleverness time lends even to young brutes.

"At 'em, boys!" he cried.

# Chapter 57

## WE GET THE OLD HEAVE HO!

Of the next twenty or thirty seconds, I can give no clear description. I can only say that we were plummeted from the office into the barroom where the flats of cleavers and bouncing billy clubs assailed us from every direction. By the time we were propelled from the front door we were a mass of bruises and bloody abrasions. When we regained our senses and looked about us, like drunken men, we saw the two Headquarters boys lying in the gutter, empulped, perhaps dying. They had been treated with special cruelty.

There was a gaping cut on Wilson's forehead that wanted some cat gut.

"I'll take Wilson and get some help," I said. "You stay here, Eddie. Keep a sharp eye. I don't want that bird flying. I'll bring an ambulance for the Headquarters boys. Looks like you were right. We're going to need lots of help."

I left Poe on his own to do what he could to protect the fallen Headquarters boys and to keep an eye on Meade's back door, and led Wilson away. He was bleeding profusely.

I asked him if he could make it.

"I'm O.K., Sarge," he said, and promptly fainted.

I lifted him on my shoulders. Perhaps because both Wilson and I were Anthony Street boys ourselves, the coppers we passed refrained from any further attack, though we were jeered as we made our way in the direction of City Hall. Near Broadway I found a hack.

I reported to Chief Matsell, who had gathered a detachment of twenty policemen. I warned him that we were at the onset of a police riot, and that we might need the intervention of the army. "The Five Points is about to blow up," I told him.

He said he would contact the military. "But I do not like the idea of the Municipal Police being saved by the United States Army," he complained, though it was nothing new.

# Chapter 58

## RIOT

I marched to Anthony Street, twenty policemen behind me, amid hoots and catcalls from Plug Uglies and Anthony Street Leatherheads alike.

The ambulance had arrived ahead of us. The hospital attendants were unaccosted as they removed the two Headquarters boys. Poe was nowhere to be seen.

We stormed the American Saloon, only to find it all but empty. A few bar flies lingered. "Where's everyone gone?" I shouted.

"Off to Paradise Square," I was told, "to hear Boss Meade make a speech." We left the American Saloon, and marched down Anthony Street toward the Square.

There we found about a thousand heavily armed gangsters, with their no less ferocious molls, and a good sprinkling of Anthony Street leatherheads, cheering the all but inaudible words of Boss Meade, who stood upon a box on a wagon amid them. He saw us, pointed at us, and shouted obscenities. The crowd turned upon us.

A disciplined detachment of police officers armed with heavy clubs, and knowing how to use them, can wreak havoc, however outnumbered. My purpose was to disperse the crowd and make my way to Meade. I told the boys to form a wedge, and, raising my club on high, cried, "Advance!"

I kept my eye on Meade as well as I could while smashing heads, left and right. It was bloody pandemonium.

Then I looked up and saw that Meade was gone. In his place was No-Nose Mullins, staring over the fray, obviously seeking out a special face in the crowd. He leaped from the wagon, ivory nose catching the sun, long hair, and scarf, flying, and made his way to the east through an animal convulsion of mob violence. Vaguely, I wondered what he was up to. I felt a shadow at my side and raised my club. Poe stopped my arm.

"Take your pistol," he cried.

I took the weapon and shoved it into my belt. "Cover your head, Poe," I shouted, "or someone, friend or foe, will bash it in!" His calm amazed me.

But things were going badly. I had at least ten Headquarters boys down. The mob, which had at first backed off, was closing in on us now. I didn't look at the faces of the men and women, I looked at their hands. Cleavers, brass knuckles, barrel staves, axes, hatchets, pitchforks, a few muskets passed under my scan.

A bugle blew the charge, and into Paradise Square from the five streets of the Five Points, the United States cavalry converged, sabres flying. The hooves of their horses trampled the fallen dead and wounded. In fifteen minutes the back of the mob was broken, and the gangsters had scattered into every rat hole and refuge of the Five Points.

228

## Chapter 59

## BAT AND RAT ALLEY

I gathered about me the remaining five able-bodied Head-quarters boys. I had seen Meade take off in the direction of the Old Brewery. I knew the rabbit warren of tunnels that lay under it, and guessed that he would try to make his escape through one of them. I had heard rumor of one tunnel that led all the way to the South Street pier. I knew that Meade kept a boat there.

A raid on the Old Brewery had never succeeded, had rarely been attempted, but things were different today. Its most vicious thugs were in the streets, fighting the cavalry. I thought: "I will be the first to bring it off!"

But not quite. For as my Headquarters boys and I entered the portals of the Old Brewery, we found Poe awaiting us. Waving for me to follow, he cried, "Down below! Follow me!" and vanished in a doorway. We followed him down to the second cellar. Again he had vanished, but his echoing voice gave us direction. We clanged over damp stone, knocking things and people aside, swinging our clubs in the dark. Ahead, a flame arced. Poe had found a torch. He stood illumined in a small doorway. The door had been torn off and lay at his feet. Above his torch was a board with the inscription *BAT AN' RAT TUNNEL* carved on it.

"He's gone in here," cried Poe. "Follow me." The stones beneath our feet were slimy with what seemed clay, or was it the screaming rats we were trampling underfoot? Frightened bats softly clubbed our heads and shoulders in their flight. So close were the quarters that we could smell their smoking wings as Poe singed them with his torch. We clamored through this subterranean hell for perhaps a city block, following the torch, when Poe dropped it, and it snuffed. From the clattering ahead I knew that he had slipped. The Headquarters boys single-filed close behind me. I came upon Poe, and helped him regain his footing in the dark. But not quite dark, now; for there was a vague light ahead, at a distance of perhaps twenty yards, and the sound of scuffling. Then came a flash. Poe's back was propelled into my chest like a cannonball, and each man behind me took the same blow. We went down like dominoes.

*Oh, God!* I thought. *Eddie's been hit!*

Then a second shot rang out.

## Chapter 60

## THE HUNTERS STALKED

My wonder at Poe knew no bounds. He was a shaman, a magician. I had felt the bullet that hit him myself, as had the men behind me, and yet he leaped to his feet and continued apace down Bat and Rat Alley. Was he made of steel? Awestruck, I picked up the chase.

There was light at the end of the tunnel where Eddie stood looking down at the body of Boss Meade, neatly plugged through the brain. The evil giant lay dead, his doppelgänger, as Eddie would say, his double, or his ghost, exited into the upper regions, known as South Street pier.

"Poe," I cried, "let me look at you." I pulled him about and looked him up and down. "How?"

"Never mind that now. Meade was ambushed by our killer. Quick! Up into the street."

I told the leatherheads to remove Meade's body to the morgue and followed Poe up into the street. Confusion of light and traffic on the street above at first made it impossible for me to gather my thoughts. I was still trying to understand how Poe took a ball in the heart to no effect. "Our killer?" Had my thoughts been at all organized, they would have amounted to *who, what, where, why*? Maybe there would have been a big HOW for exclamation point. I blurted, "Wasn't Boss Meade behind everything?"

"No!"

"Then it was the man who ambushed him?"

"Yes."

"But he can't be found. Look at this street."

"Quite a crowd, isn't it?" said Poe. "But we don't have to find him. We're as magnets to him. If we draw away, he will be compelled to follow." Poe hailed a coach. "Quick, aboard!" he said to me; and to the coachman, "The Phoenix Theatre, at your leisure."

"Sir, the Phoenix Theatre was just burnt to the ground. There'll be no theatricals there for a while."

"I beg to differ, my good man. I am expecting to see something between a tragedy and a farce. *On*, as I say!"

# Chapter 61

## POE SPRINGS THE TRAP

As the coachman left us, in front of the Phoenix Theatre, I distinctly heard him say, "Rid of another madman. How many more tonight?"

About twenty-five yards into Phoenix Alley, I heard footsteps behind us. My hackles rose as we clanged over the cobbles. "Poe," I said.

"Yes, there he is now, right on time for his final performance," said Poe, who looked intense and sounded gleeful. "Be on the ready. Judging by his performance in the park, I don't think he's a very good shot."

"But he hit *you*—didn't he?"

"He was aiming at Meade. It took him two shots and he was close upon his target. Keep about twenty feet distance from him and you have little to fear."

As if proving Poe's point, a ball ricocheted with several twangs against the close-set buildings that walled the alley.

"We have him now," cried Poe.

"Have *him!* He has *us!*" I turned and discharged my pistol only to be answered with another shot.

"Damn those repeating pistols!" I cried.

"Run," said Poe, needlessly, for I was running. "We'll catch him when he comes out."

"Who, for God's sake!"

"Why, Mullins, of course. Quickly, now!"

Mullins fired again. "We won't make it to the end of the alley," I cried. "Find the door! Find the door!"

"Here, here," cried Poe.

I ran by him. He reached out and pulled me in. We threw our weight against the fire-weakened door. It gave easily.

We found ourselves in a dark passage. There were stairs. We climbed them and groped toward a patch of light that showed the beautiful wide stage.

"We're on stage. The sundown is our limelight," said Poe. But he vanished in the dark.

"Poe!" I called.

"Here," came a voice.

I turned.

Mullins advanced toward me in the dim light, a top-hatted, ivory-nosed giant lifting a gleaming cleaver above me. I fell backward. The cleaver was poised to strike. *I was a dead man!*

234

There was a swoosh, a cry, and then there was nothing but the jagged light and dark of the burnt-out hollow of the theatre. Death had vanished before my eyes.

I jumped when Poe touched my shoulder.

"Where did he go?" I asked, bewildered.

"Through the trap door," said Poe. "I gave him the hook, so to speak. Now let's go down and pick that bad actor up, shall we?"

# Chapter 62

## THE HERO

We had crowded into Red Kate's bedroom to welcome VanBrunt home from the hospital. His head was still bandaged, but the bandage looked like a turban, and his aspect was that of a lugubrious sheik. He was pillowed-up in Red Kate's baldaquined bed, wearing the silver silk, gold-initialed dressing gown, which Kate had given him as a coming home present, and across his lap sat a silver bedtray with a silver coffee pot and toast holder, and a beautiful China cup and saucer. Red Kate was sparing no expense in his honor. He held up *The Broadway Star* before us. The headlines read:

### VANBRUNT CLEARED, BOSS MEADE DEAD

"Well done," cried VanBrunt. He beamed upon the gathering. "Listen," he said, and began reading, "'Horrible discoveries were made in the aftermath of the raid on the Old Brewery. The bodies of over fifty men, women, and children, many mere skeletons, others in various states of decomposition, and some showing signs of recent death, were discovered by the Army medical team that entered after the riot. Many of the bodies were found superficially buried in the walls and floors of the building. At least half showed signs of violent death.'"

He crumpled the newspaper and let it fall by the bed. "Kiss me, Kate," he said in a quick burst of exuberance, and she

236

accommodated him with a buss on the lips. He was her man, it seemed, poor flawed fellow that he was.

"Wretched business," I said. "Perhaps we'll get the Old Brewery cleaned out at last."

VanBrunt was completely sober for the first time since I'd known him. Sobriety made him twitch. When he twitched, Red Kate, who sat on a chair beside the bed, patted his arm maternally. He turned his red, white, and blue eyes from Kate to Poe and myself, who stood on the other side of the bed from Kate.

"Peter must stay in bed for two weeks," said Kate, patting his arm, "but he's going to be fine. I'll be opening my new hotel next month, and everything is going to be different. It's on the Bowery, very fashionable right now, up near Washington Square, quite respectable. Peter is going to be my manager, and I'm going to bask in the straight life. It's what I've yearned for these . . .well . . .many years. It'll be good to have a real gentleman as my manager. It'll be a big step for all of us."

"My dear friend," said Poe to VanBrunt, "you have been nothing but a worry to me." He smiled. "I'm so glad to see you. . . almost on your feet."

"My family had forsaken me," said VanBrunt, "and really I thought I had no friend in the world, but now I feel as if surrounded by a friendly family. Dear Kate, Sergeant Goode, and you, Eddie."

"I am something of a black sheep myself," said Poe. "But do not think, because thou has taken to virtue, there shall be no

237

more cakes and ale. By which I mean—when you are managing Kate's respectable hotel—give entry to, and suffer, a wanton poet, should he appear at your door."

"Oh, always, Eddie!" said Red Kate.

"And Mr. O'Brien," said VanBrunt, "through Dr. Whitney's kind offices, has now taken me up—so there are two more friends."

"What does Mr. O'Brien say?" I asked.

"Well, when I came to in the hospital, he was right there, with a private doctor—all taken care of by Dr. Whitney— and they brought me here, as I asked. O'Brien had gotten a writ of habeas corpus, based on lack of evidence, and here I am. He says that I will never see the inside of a cell again. He says that I shouldn't have been arrested at all."

"Did you know that Eddie was shot?" I asked.

"*Eddie!*" cried Kate.

"I wasn't hurt," said Poe. "I was carrying a Bible in a large pocket inside my cape. The ball was stopped by it, only penetrating about halfway in. It knocked the wind out of me, however."

"And the rest of us behind you," I said.

"What were you doing with a Bible?" asked VanBrunt.

"I had picked it up from a bookbinder's on our return from Fordham. I had it rebound for a friend, and now I am afraid that I shall have to have it rebound again, or replaced. The ball is still in it, having come to rest at 'Jesus wept'!"

I knew that Eddie was being dramatic—what an assertion!

"It would be quite a memento," said VanBrunt. "Offer it back to your friend as it is and see what he thinks."

"*She*," said Poe. "It's the property of a lady. Perhaps I should do so, with the story attached, as I can't afford any more bindings."

"When we returned from Fordham," I told VanBrunt, "my first thought was of you, to see how you fared, and also to ask you what happened at the Old Brewery. But when I reported to Headquarters, they were holding a warrant for the arrest of Meade. I found Eddie just back from the bookbinder's, and we went right on to Meade's American Saloon. Tell me now, what *did* happen at the Old Brewery that night?"

## Chapter 63

## THE KILLER'S CONK

VanBrunt shifted his position to think. "I don't remember very clearly. Let me see. I was talking to Max Fisch, and he told me he knew where the Gimp could be found, and he'd take me there, if I wanted to confront the boy, and ask him why he was accusing me. I know, of course, that I should not have gone. But I was drunk. Max Fisch took me to the Old Brewery. We went to a small room on the ground floor—"

"Not the room where you and the Gimp were found?" I asked.

"No, no. It was a tiny room, no bigger than a pantry, not in the basement, where they say we were found, but on the ground floor."

"How can you be sure?" asked Poe.

"Some things I remember, others I don't. But why is it important?"

"Because Max Fisch wasn't strong enough to have carried you to the basement. He can't weigh more than a hundred pounds. Of course, he could have gotten some Old Brewery cutthroats to carry you down. Do you remember being hit?"

"No."

240

"Do you see," said Poe, "the question is, did Max Fisch take you there to rob you, or for some other reason, involving someone else? But go on."

"Well, there were a table and two old chairs. Fisch took the one facing the door, across from me, and I sat with my back to the door. Then he brought out a bottle of rum and poured us each a drink. I asked him where the boy was. He said that the boy would come in good time. We talked—about Mary Hart. The murder. Then we sang some songs. But that's all I remember. Nothing more until I woke up in the hospital four days ago. When I first woke up, I just thought I had a hang-over, my head was pounding so."

"Either you were already unconscious from the drink and struck anyway, or you were in such a fog that you didn't know you were struck," said Poe. "In any case, you were moved, and someone was there with Max Fisch."

"Our ivory-conked friend," I said. As Eddie put it to me—he has a great sense of humor, you know—in order to find our killer, all we had to do was follow his nose."

# Chapter 64

## I BECOME FAMOUS

Poe vanished before the trial, having told me that he wanted no part of it. He had insisted that I take full credit for the capture of Brody-Mullins, who, by the way, had broken a leg when he fell through the trap door. Poe had also put Russell McNeil on his honor not to mention his name in the newspaper reports of the case McNeil was publishing in *The Broadway Star*. Therefore, when McNeil later published his book, *The Butcher*, composed from the newspaper pieces, I was its hero. In light of such publicity, my temporary, and highly political, appointment as captain was made permanent. And so it was that I became a famous detective.

## Chapter 65

## I INHERIT

During Brody's trial, in which I played so prominent a role, an element, as it were, out of the blue, added to my public notice. At long last, I was awarded a large sum by the Maritime Insurance Company, which held the policy on my father's schooner. The sum was adequate to insure my independence, and I decided to propose to Eleanor Whitney, who, by the grace of God, accepted; as, I might add, did the society set. Indeed, circumstances had so altered my standing, that, rather than our engagement causing a scandal, it was looked upon as a romantic *cause célèbre*. My inheritance alone would not have achieved this; it was merely the element required to validate my public standing. It was a season in which several New York heiresses had run off with their coachmen, and I suppose I looked good by comparison.

# Chapter 66

## P. T. BARNUM

For two weeks after the trial and before the execution, Gothamites flocked to the tombs to get a look at the multiple murderer. Among those to visit Brody was one Phineas T. Barnum, the great showman. Barnum asked for a conference with Brody, which Chief Matsell granted. He then informed Brody that he wished for certain of his possessions, including, most specially, his ivory nose, which was to be placed on a wax figure of Brody, cleaver raised on high, in the act of killing a Hot Corn girl. The figure was to be on permanent display in Barnum's American Museum on Broadway. In return for his concessions, the impresario promised Brody good food and cigars unlimited until the time set for his execution, a new suit, including an expensive plug hat, to wear at that event, and the most lavish funeral yet given to a Gotham gangster. Brody accepted.

# Chapter 67

## SKULLDUGGERY

At exactly eleven thirty, on Friday, June 16, 1848, Brody stepped on the death platform. After he exchanged handshakes with Mr. Barnum, Chief Matsell, myself, and others, the rope was cut and Brody's great body dropped through a trap that broke his neck rather than his leg. He was interred in Calvary Cemetery, at Barnum's expense, and a marble headstone was erected with the inscription:

*JOSEPH BRODY - 1812-1848*

*BUTCHER AND MASS MURDERER*

*RESTLESS UNTIL FORGIVEN*

The words were prophetic, for, within a week, Brody's body was sold to medical students by grave robbers. An intern at the City Hospital recognized the famous noseless cadaver, the ghouls were tracked down and arrested, and the body was re-buried, this time in potter's field, Barnum rejecting any further expense. The headstone remains over the empty grave.

# Chapter 68

## OUR ENGAGEMENT DINNER

On July 7th, 1848, Eleanor and I gave a dinner party at her house on Washington Square, its purpose being to formalize our engagement and to see again those friends who had played such a part in the affair which had brought us together. Poe arrived at my boarding house on Greenwich Street on the 5th, two days before, and just after the July 4th celebration. He was a bit worse for wear, and needed some tending and rest before the appointed evening.

After the celebratory dinner and several toasts "to the happy couple," we sat at the table and listened as Russell McNeil finished reading aloud from his popular account of Joe Brody's life and death, *The Butcher*.

"It's a good piece," said Fleetwood O'Brien. "I read it when it was first published in *The Broadway Star*."

"I'm amazed," said McNeil, "that neither you, Captain Goode, nor Dr. Whitney—nor you, Mr. Poe—have read it."

"I was still too shaken by those events," said Eleanor. "I did not wish to remind myself that that butcher had invaded my very home."

"I was in Philadelphia," said Poe.

I shrugged and lit a cigar. "I was there."

Eleanor excused herself and went upstairs. She returned in a few minutes, saying: "Danny's sleeping peacefully, little tad. Did you know that we are going to adopt him, Eddie, as soon as Jon and I are married?"

"Jon told me, yes. Congratulations on that as well. You are all—Jon, yourself, and the boy—quite fortunate. Of course, Jon is the most fortunate."

"Thank you, Eddie," said Eleanor. "You know, I still don't really grasp it all. I thought Meade was behind the whole thing. I suppose it was my own self-righteousness that deluded me."

"Meade had nothing directly to do with any of it," I said. "But McNeil here has written the story. Let him explain it."

"But it is from you," said McNeil, "that much of it comes. *You* explain it."

I said: "*You* interviewed Brody."

McNeil said: "But there are still details to be cleared up. Eddie told me several things that Brody confirmed. But—"

"Why not let Eddie explain it?" I said. "He's our great story-teller, and actually did most of the imaginative work on the case. Ratiocination—do ye call it, Eddie?"

## Chapter 69

## LUCY HART AND THE DIARY

"Reasoning, or the process of exact thinking; also, a piece of reasoning. Notice that I would differentiate between ratiocination and logic, which is a bound system and fails in that it is exclusive of human nature. From the beginning, then:

"Joe Brody had been a criminal since his childhood. The same might have been Danny's fate, had you two not intervened. Joe Brody's profession was that of petty gangster. He had probably murdered before the first case of which I am aware—murder was nothing to him, a condition of survival, that was all—and he probably would have murdered—perhaps many times again, had not Jon brought his career to an end. He was ignorant but cunning, and being the brute this world had made him, was merely trying to protect himself. He did not realize that the murder of Mary Hart and the accusation against VanBrunt would be of such interest to the world outside Paradise Square, where murder often went like the orphan of interest.

"The first murder that he committed of which I am aware was the murder of his wife, Lucy. But, as I say, he undoubtedly murdered before, so none of these subsequent misdeeds, dire as they were, can, I think, through his eyes, be seen in as monstrous a light as they are through ours.

"It was through the description of what occurred on the Sunday morning that they picked Brody up, given us by the

Butchers at the fortification, that I first came to sense what had happened to Lucy Hart. The Butchers, so far as I could see, had no reason to lie, particularly as they had no intention of letting us escape, and they said that they found Brody sitting on a chair at the kitchen table next to his wife's body, which lay on the floor. They said that the room was quite cold but that the body was putrid. In a cold apartment, it would take some time to have reached such a state. Yet we know that Lucy was alive on the Friday night previous, for it was then that Joe Brody was taunted with her infidelity with Meade and went home to confront her. I had assumed for some time that he killed her that night, giving two days, more or less, until Sunday, when the Butchers found her in the condition described. This McNeil has had confirmed by Brody himself.

"It went like this: Brody and Lucy had a fight. Brody was drunk, hurt, angry, and felt like a fool for allowing himself to be misused by both his wife and his boss, Meade. Lucy, who usually could command his respect, for he thought of her as superior to himself in that she had had some education, could read and write, as he once put it, was afraid of him now. She *had* been keeping a record of her encounters with Meade—probably as an insurance policy should Meade toss her aside as he was wont to do with his women. The story of Meade's treatment of Red Kate was well known in the Five Points. Now Lucy decided to distract her husband's slow mind with news of this record, her diary, and to bring him into collusion with her against Meade; for the worst had happened, from her viewpoint, and Meade had announced that he was through with her only a few days before.

"She told Brody that she had such a diary, but she did not let him see it. In fact, it was already hidden, thought to be a

249

Bible, and held in her blind mother's hands. She had hidden it earlier that day.

"But Brody was implacable, furious. He killed her with one blow of his cleaver.

"Then he got an idea. If Lucy had kept a diary, and he could find it, he could use it against Meade, not merely out of revenge, but for profit as well. He proceeded to search for the diary. But not finding it, he doubted its existence, thinking now that Lucy was only pretending to have such a document in order to distract him. Then he was inspired. He decided to pretend that the diary existed and to threaten Meade with it, to see what he could get. He was drinking heavily, and probably slept for several hours at some point here.

"Lucy, during her harangue, mentioned our friend, here, Mr. McNeil, the reformer journalist, who would like to get something on Meade. On Saturday afternoon, leaving Lucy's body where it had fallen, he went to you, McNeil, to test the water, as it were. He told you his business, said that he had some evidence, and, as an appetizer, told about that part of Meade's background involving Red Kate. This was interesting, but you wanted solid evidence. Brody told you about the diary. Was that solid enough? This exchange was overheard by someone in your office, a spy for Meade. This is why Meade did not doubt Brody when Brody told him that he had been to *The Broadway Star*.

"Upon leaving you, and after stopping for a few additional drinks, Brody presented himself to Meade. He told Meade what he knew about Meade and Lucy, and about Lucy's diary, wherein she told all about Meade's crooked deals, to

250

which she had been privy because Meade thought of her as being as harmless and brainless as a doll.

"Meade, uncertain what to believe, but having the confirmation of his own spy that Brody had been to *The Broadway Star*, played along for a time, asking what Brody wanted for the diary. Brody said that he wanted one hundred dollars, not having any idea what to ask for because he had no idea what such a diary, if indeed it existed, would be worth.

"Meade must have thought the sum a ridiculous one for so valuable a piece of evidence. He told Brody that he would pay him the money when the diary was produced, and gave him a day to produce it.

"It was Saturday night. Brody stopped to have a few more drinks, and then went home to ransack the place a second time, to no avail. He then sat down next to his wife's body and drank himself into oblivion.

"Waking Sunday morning, he was again inspired. Maybe Lucy had given the diary to Mrs. Hart, or maybe she had hidden it in Mrs. Hart's room. He knew, for Mrs. Hart was strict in this observance, that Mary Hart, his teenage sister-in-law, for whom he felt the most unbrotherly feelings, took her blind mother to church at the mission at eleven o'clock every Sunday morning.

"He waited until he saw Mary take her mother off to church, and then broke in and ransacked their rooms, breaking into the chest, but taking no note of the coverless Bible therein. He could not know that the blind woman was actually carrying the diary, in its Bible cover, with her as she passed out of his sight. *She* did not even know it. Of course, he

251

found nothing and returned to his own rooms, where he was discovered by the gangsters—whom we met, Jon—Legs and Butt.

"They saw that he had killed his wife. This did not overly surprise them, as they had been among those who had taunted him with his wife's infidelity. They searched for the diary themselves, found nothing, and returned with him to Boss Meade, who now believed that Brody had attempted to hoax him. That Lucy Hart Brody was dead meant nothing to Meade, but that he was ultimately rid of her. But Brody's threat must be punished. The Butchers cut off his nose.

# Chapter 70

## JOE BRODY A.K.A NO-NOSE MULLINS

"Brody spent a couple of days in the hospital, left wearing a bandage, vanished, and returned a year later, now wearing that ivory nose, long hair and a beard, and looking altogether unlike his former self, except, of course, for size.

"He knew of Red Kate's hatred of Meade, so, without much effort, he became her major domo. She was unaware of his background.

"Mary Hart was a year older now. She had become a Hot Corn Girl and was becoming a very lovely young lady. Her charms were widely noticed by men. No-Nose Mullins noticed her, as he had earlier. He made advances and was rejected, for Mary recognized and hated him. Her hatred served to increase, inflame, his passion for her.

"He would go to the mission and wait to see her. Several times she was compelled to talk to him, so as not to cause trouble. Nor did she want her mother to know that he was alive. He himself had been surprised to discover, upon his return to the city, that it was generally believed that the Butcher's Gang had killed Lucy Hart Brody and that he, in his former incarnation as Joe Brody, was also thought to be dead, another victim of the Butcher's Gang.

"His pursuit of Mary Hart went on sporadically for nearly four years. This brings in Thorndyke, as I will explain in a few moments. Finally, in part because it was true and in part to be rid of Mullins, Mary Hart told him that she would marry Peter VanBrunt, if he proposed. She described Van Brunt to Mullins, not aware that Mullins already knew him.

"That night at Red Kate's bar, when VanBrunt told Mullins and others of his intention to meet with Mary Hart in Paradise Square, by prearrangement, and to propose to her, Mullins, driven by violent jealousy, took cleaver in hand and followed VanBrunt. But VanBrunt stopped at several diving bells on his way to the park.

"Mullins went ahead, unknown by VanBrunt, to confront Mary Hart. Their confrontation resulted in her death. Whether he left the cleaver by the body with some vague design to place the blame at the door of the Butcher's Gang, is not quite clear. He seems to have had that in mind.

"But, as he left the park, he ran into the Gimp, and the Gimp knew what had occurred. Mary Hart's scream had brought people. It was dark. Mullins seized the Gimp, warning him to be quiet. It was just then that VanBrunt entered the park at the opposite gate, and kneeled down by Mary, taking her up in his arms. As he knelt, not seeing anything but his dead angel, he felt the cleaver at his knee and took it in hand.

"Mullins told the frightened Gimp to say only that what he now saw—VanBrunt, the body, and the cleaver—was all he knew of the crime, on threat of horrible death if he didn't and a reward of money if he did. So much for the Gimp's strange willingness to talk. Mullins mingled in the crowd. But one other person knew that VanBrunt probably did not commit the murder—that was Danny Devlin, who heard

254

Mary Hart scream and *then* saw VanBrunt hasten toward that scream."

"Then we came into the picture," I said. "Red Kate sent Mullins with us. He must have been afraid, for he knew we meant to question the Gimp, and the Gimp might give him away, but he also *wished* to go with us, to be on the spot, as it were, and to know what progress we were making."

"You, Jon," Poe continued, "observed, as you commented upon, the strange looks the Gimp and Mullins exchanged, but we attributed that exchange to their ignorance and to the fact that both were deformed, the foot and the face, and thought little of it. What we were seeing, however, was the shock of recognition.

"We adjourned to the diving bell, as you will remember. I was in a weakened condition and in need of fortification. We sent Mullins back to the park, if you can call it that, to get the Gimp. Instead of getting the Gimp, he warned him away.

"But my offer of reward for information to be brought to me at the diving bell had the result of bringing Danny Devlin to us.

"When Mullins observed my skill with mesmerism, my ability to make the boy tell the truth, for Danny would not have done so otherwise, he became very frightened of me, and his hatred of me began there, as it often does, in fear. I had succeeded in showing you that VanBrunt was very likely innocent of the charge against him. Mullins decided that he had work to do. He must get rid of me at the first

255

opportunity, for sooner or later, he feared, I would get at the truth.

"That night VanBrunt was free. We retired. Thank God that I took your advice and example, when you told me that you always sleep under the bed rather than on it when you were in a dangerous place."

# Chapter 71

## MAX FISCH AND THE GIMP

"Mullins, alone with Max Fisch, the perfect person to blame my intended death upon, improvised. He told Max Fisch to tell VanBrunt where the Gimp could be found and to encourage our, by then, drunken friend, to confront his accuser and to get the truth from him. VanBrunt went along.

"He and Max Fisch went to the Old Brewery. Fisch took him to a room suggested by Mullins, who had lived in the Old Brewery when young and knew it well, and got Van-Brunt to sit with his back to the door—an easy task for Fisch, all of this, really, as VanBrunt was quite drunk. Fisch had been told that he would be rewarded. Perhaps he thought that Mullins meant to rob VanBrunt. He knew nothing about the inter-relationships involved.

"Mullins blackjacked VanBrunt from behind, his purpose being only to knock him out for a short time so that Van-Brunt would seem to have killed the Gimp and then to have passed out drunk. Then Mullins had Fisch help him with VanBrunt. They took him downstairs to the room in which you found me on that Wednesday morning, Jon, where the Gimp lay sleeping and put VanBrunt at the table. Mullins then strangled the Gimp. Then he strangled Fisch, took Fisch's initialed and well-known pistol from him, and carried little Max off to another room, dropping him in a barrel. He only desired that Max not be found for a day or two—long enough so that he could still be blamed for attempting to rob me, and for my murder.

257

# Chapter 72

## ATTEMPTED MURDER

"Mullins returned to Kate's, came up the back hall stairs to my door, opened it, and, he thought, shot me. He threw the initialed pistol on the floor and went to the back fire stairs, out, down, around to the front, and came up with Red Kate to find me alive. It must have been a shock to him. He probably had himself convinced by now that I had supernatural powers. My survival was only one of the things that he didn't, could not foresee. And he did not get another good chance to kill me until he followed us into a trap, and ultimately, to his own doom."

"Why did he murder poor Mr. Thorndyke?" asked Eleanor. "Surely he was no threat to . . . anyone."

"He killed Thorndyke because Thorndyke could associate him with Mary Hart. He had visited Thorndyke on the pretense of receiving spiritual ministrations, but actually in order to contact the Hot Corn Girl who was his passion. But here his ever-inspired mind played him badly false."

## Chapter 73

## THADEUS THORNDYKE AND DANNY DEVLIN

Poe seemed lost in thought for a moment. He stood by his place at the table, looking at each of us. "After murdering Thorndyke he lurked about," he said, "waiting to see where we would go next. He knew Danny was at the mission and he didn't want to let the boy out of his sight. His limited brain was by this time heavily overtaxed. His very first impulse had been to attempt to place blame on the Butcher's Gang, whom he hated, because they had both disgraced and disfigured him, for Mary Hart's murder, as he had managed to place public blame on them for Lucy's death. Then the opportunity presented itself to blame Mary's death on VanBrunt. He seized it. But he couldn't blame Thorndyke's death on VanBrunt, because VanBrunt was in the hospital unconscious, due to his own, Mullins's, over-zealous blow to VanBrunt's head.

"He knew that we had begun to suspect the Butcher Boss Meade and his gang, so he reverted to that, leaving that semi-literate note on Thorndyke's chest, claiming for the Butcher's Gang even the murder of Mary Hart.

"Nevertheless, confused, afraid, he wasn't certain that Danny Devlin might not be a danger to him, being able, as he was, to show that VanBrunt was probably *not* the murderer.

"He must cover everything, for he could no longer follow the thread of evidence himself. So he followed you to this very house. He saw you, Eleanor, light up Danny's room and put him to bed. He watched from Washington Square, across the street. But he would not make an attempt on Danny then, for he wanted to blame the Plug Uglies once again, if he should be seen, and he needed his costume, plus a scarf to hide his nose. Brody reasoned a Plug Ugly might be identified as a Plug Ugly, not as an individual. After all, there are hundreds of Plug Uglies. Further, he knew that I was probably back at Red Kate's, and he wanted to hurry back because he knew that his absence would be noticed and you would soon be looking for him there as well.

"He told us that he had spent his time away looking for Max Fisch. Later, he told us that little Max had been seen. This was pure obscuration.

"The night of the dinner party was the perfect time for him to strike at Danny, tucked away in bed, all the adults downstairs, and everybody, including the servants, busy, preoccupied."

"What about Meade's demise?" asked Eleanor.

"Mullins saw an opportunity to kill the man who had had him mutilated, and took it. He had no intention of helping us. It was mere chance that his action should save us. I imagine that, if he had known Meade had us dead in his sights, he'd have let Meade shoot us first, then would have killed him." Poe shrugged. "You know the rest."

"Ably recounted," said McNeil. "I suppose you intend to write a version of it yourself, to compete with my official version."

"No," said Poe, ever the contrarian. "It's not my kind of story."

"But, dear friends," I said, "it certainly is *my* kind of story."

Capt. Jonathan Goode
New York Municipal Police, 1851

CPSIA information can be obtained
at www.ICGtesting.com
Printed in the USA
BVHW030953050719
552688BV00002B/11/P